Praise for Kathryn Davis

"Davis, God bless her, assumes her readers are intelligent . . . people who are interested in what they are reading."

— Ann Patchett, *Mirabella*

"Davis's writing is so extraordinarily visual that she is practically a video artist."

— *The New Yorker*

"Davis . . . seems equal parts Jane Austen and Isak Dinesen. . . . One of the most thoroughly original (and valuable) of contemporary writers."

— *Kirkus Reviews*

"I cannot say how much I admire Kathryn Davis . . . brilliant in every way, and often delightfully funny."

— Sigrid Nunez, author of *For Rouenna*

"Kathryn Davis never fails to astonish with her fiction. . . . She leads us deep into the great mysteries of human ambition, love, and restlessness. It's a dazzling journey."

— Joanna Scott, author of *Tourmaline*

"Kathryn Davis's books not only defy easy description, but tend to elicit inadequate book-chat clichés like 'hypnotic' and 'haunting' to convey their astonishing effects. Davis's approach to novel-writing is so original, and the results so magical, that trying to review her fiction in a thousand words on a tight deadline feels as doomed as trying to review . . . one of your own dreams." — A. O. Scott, *Newsday*

"Davis is brilliant at depicting the manners and motives of her characters." — Suzanne Freeman, *Boston Globe*

"Davis can make hairpin turns in tone, from the flip . . . to the eerily lyric." — Joy Katz, *Bookforum*

"I like to think of Kathryn Davis as the love child of Virginia Woolf and Lewis Carroll, with a splash of Nabokov, Emily Brontë, and Angela Carter in the gene pool." — Joy Press, *Village Voice*

"Kathryn Davis is brilliant." — Penelope Fitzgerald, author of *The Blue Flower*

HELL

ALSO BY KATHRYN DAVIS

Labrador
The Girl Who Trod on a Loaf
The Walking Tour
Versailles

HELL

a novel by

Kathryn Davis

BACK BAY BOOKS

Little, Brown and Company

Boston   New York   London

Originally published in hardcover by The Ecco Press, 1998
First Back Bay paperback edition, September 2003

A portion of the present work appeared in a slightly different version in *Common Knowledge* (Fall 1994).

LIBRARY OF CONGRESS CATALOGING-IN-PUBLICATION DATA

Davis, Kathryn.
    Hell: a novel / by Kathryn Davis.
        p.   cm.
    ISBN 0-88001-560-8 (hc) / 0-316-73505-1 (pb)
    1. Title.
PS3554.A934923H45   1998
813'.54 — dc21   97-17326

10 9 8 7 6 5 4 3 2 1

Q-FF

Designed by Susanna Gilbert, The Typeworks

Printed in the United States of America

For my sister

My dear, my dear, O dear
It was an accident.

        — W. B. YEATS

HELL

SOMETHING IS WRONG IN THE HOUSE.

Of course you're dismayed. You have every right to be, for haven't you followed the rules to the letter, ridding your rooms of all corruption, the mite-infested cheese, the flyblown mutton, the sour bed linens, the dung-caked boots? You've sponged the floors, beaten the rugs, hung rue at the threshold; a fire is burning briskly in the kitchen, a pudding chilling in the pantry on its bed of ice. Yet how can it be that when you permit yourself a moment's relaxation, standing at the window you washed only yesterday, its panes don't reflect back the bright prospect of a clear conscience, but the treacherous face of the world?

And what's the use, really, if you can no longer tell the difference? What's the use if you can no longer tell where your face leaves off and the gray sky begins? Raindrops stream down the window, ruining your hard work. That yellow-haired girl peeking from between the trees on the other side of the mill-race, spying on a delicate yellow leaf caught trembling in an eddy—can that be poor Joy Harbison, or is it some other lively figment, anachronism or memory, ghost or invention?

In the beginning, we're told, everything *was* the same. Everything was locked together inside a huge lump of ice. But soon enough the ice began to melt, and because it was too huge to notice the moistly fraying hem of itself, threads of milky silt-filled water unraveled across the landscape, slowly at first, then fast, faster, setting the miller's wheel in motion, thundering toward a future where a little yellow leaf was sweeping over the lip of the dam. Rain was falling from a sky that spectral shade of gray that's almost white, dispiriting, and I was sitting at my father's bedside, eating fries out of a paper bag.

Something's wrong, my father was saying to my mother. I can feel it in my bones. Did you turn off the stove? One of these days you're going to burn down the house, Dorothy. Eat your lunch, Edwin, she replied. Ever since his stroke my mother had been on top, but now my father was going to get the upper hand by starving himself to death. Out the window mountains, clouds, a landscape as featureless and vast as the hospital room we were in was cramped and populous. Out the window Nature, and is that where you're headed when you're dying? Or is the afterworld as crowded as Napoleon's table at Malmaison, beautiful women, jabbering men, Antonin Carême's brilliant pyramids of food?

In my father's room there were white take-out bags on the bedtray, fries and soft drinks and burgers, though it hardly mattered to him. After the stroke he could only see half of everything: his plate, his hand, his face. The moral vision, similarly bisected, becomes strangely severe.

Gold will suffer, my father said, but it will serve him right. That poor little kid, whatever happened to her? Little Blondie, you know the one I mean, he said, letting out a long slow whistle while pointing over his shoulder with his thumb, a gesture we all knew meant "flew the coop." When it's no longer your job to carve the empire, rule the kingdom, balance the scales of justice, often the best position left open is that of prophet.

He'll turn to salt if the earthworms don't get him first, my father added. X marks the spot.

I haven't the faintest idea what you're talking about, Edwin, my mother replied.

Out the window the town of X, all the houses haunted, even the meanest of them, for it's common knowledge misery breeds tenacity—just ask my mother. The houses haunted and the pond perfectly smooth, except near the dance pavilion where someone has just stood, wobbled for a moment, dizzy, to wade through the sickeningly hot water at the pond's edge, leaving a fan of black creases. A strand of bright green algae wrapping around one ankle. A barking dog. The ruined chimneys of Moss Cottage looking down like sentinels, all that remain of the shake-shingled hideaway where Edwina Moss delivered herself of the single endless sentence that was to be her last word on household management, after she lost her husband, her daughter, her mind.

SOMETHING IS WRONG IN THE HOUSE. There's always something wrong in the house.

Though you'd never know from the outside, the ivy-laced brick facade with its copper-roofed bow window, the white front door with its fanlight and brass knocker, the crimson azaleas bordering the stoop. And even if you were able to see inside, to swing open one whole wall, what you'd find would no doubt confirm your first impression. A mother and father, two girls, a dog, a bird. Rooms filled with mahogany furniture, soft pale drapes, glinting mirrors; cream-colored walls hung with horticultural prints in Florentine frames, *Malus pumila*, Northern Spy, Seek-no-further, Lady Sweet. A silent butler. A kid glove. Sheet music—"Night and Day" (yellow and black) or "Stairway to Heaven" (silver and red)—open on the piano, sunlight penetrating the breakfront's diamond-shaped panes to illuminate the highball glasses with their etched portraits of hunting dogs. Sometimes Fred Astaire or a mouse hanging upside down in the porthole-shaped screen of the television (the first on the block, the father's a salesman), sometimes little beads of water hanging from the glass lid of the dishwasher, also the first on the block. If on the one hand there's an essential lack of gravity about the father, there is also a thematic consistency to his choice of products.

In the kitchen the mother is poised over the stove, fixing lunch. She turns the burner up high, waits for the coils to become orange, then salts the cast-iron skillet. You want to keep the pan hot and dry when cooking hamburgers; the meat has enough fat on its own, and the quicker you sear it (Liebig's method, popular in the fifties), the tighter you seal in the juices. Of course a gas range would be preferable, but this one came with the house and was, after all, brand-new, a Hotpoint.

The mother's only making three hamburgers, because the older of her two daughters (in bed reading *Wuthering Heights*, not a wink of light coming through the venetian blinds) has refused to eat much of anything ever since she watched hamburger fall in worms from the grinder at Caruso's Market, whereas the younger daughter (pushing Tiny Tears down the upstairs hall in a blue stroller) doesn't really mind hamburger but would probably prefer peanut butter and jelly.

Let's say it's a little before noon on a Saturday in June, St. John's Eve to be exact (even though a foul wind sweeps across the moors, lifting the riders' cloaks behind them like black wings; even though it's cold and dark and snow is falling). The father is on his knees, working the soil at the back of the garden prior to setting in a flat of marigold seedlings. When the mother releases the chain that opens the vent over the stove and the exhaust fan starts up with its usual loud clanking, both the sound and the smell alert him that lunch will soon be ready. He rises slowly, first shifting his weight on one side from his right knee to his right foot, then balancing with his left hand until he's standing straight, brushing his hands on his twill work-pants.

The grass in the backyard is deep green, neatly mowed. The dachshund is lying in a pool of blackish green shade under the dogwood tree which finished blooming weeks ago, while the roses are only beginning to unfurl their red and peach and yellow petals. A trolley travels north up Germantown Avenue, sparks hissing from its cable. The parakeet is pecking away at its cuttlebone.

Something wrong here? Of course it's natural to feel apprehension anytime the picture seems flooded with light.

Through the little window over the sink the mother watches the father strike a pose not unlike that of the terracotta Saint Francis in the birdbath, his dark head bent in reflection on the rosebushes, on the exquisitely beautiful yet malign Japanese beetle creeping out of Mamie Eisenhower's peach folds. You saw me, the mother says aloud, angrily flattening the burgers (which she calls "meat-cakes" when they're served bunless) with her spatula, an unfortunate practice that tends to compress and toughen the fiber of the beef, just as it's an unfortunate quirk of design that permits sound to travel through the heat ducts from the kitchen to the older daughter's bedroom, causing her to hear not only the sizzling of burgers but her mother's voice emerging from the grate under her closet door.

You saw me and don't go pretending you didn't, the mother's voice says, though the mealybug-infested African violet in the Italian cachepot, and the wire basket crammed with hollow garlic heads, not to mention the rest of the windowsill's dust-and-grease-caked clutter (this being one of several areas the cleaning lady avoids every Tuesday) provide impediment enough, not to mention the way the sun shines directly into the father's eyes when he looks back toward the house. You know I'm watching you, the mother's voice says. You want me to see how sad you look.

Sizzle sizzle. The refrigerator door opens, slams shut. "On that bleak hilltop the earth was hard with a black frost, and the air made me shiver ..." The older daughter tries plugging her ears with her fingers, but then it's impossible to turn the pages. The smell of scorched meat drifts up the stairs.

"Beef is an exhaustless mine in the hands of a skilful artist, and is truly the king of the kitchen," wrote Antonin Carême (1784–1833), Napoleon's brilliant chef and author of *L'Art de la cuisine au dix-neuvième siècle.* "Without it no soup, no gravy; and its absence would produce almost a famine in the civilized world!"

"It has been said that when you burn food that might otherwise have been eaten," wrote Edwina Moss (1820–1864), renowned expert on household management and author of *The Blancmange,* "you will have to pick it out of hell-fire when you die."

The mother taps at the window to let the father know his lunch is ready; she wants him to see the expression on her face and concede defeat. She has him beat by a mile, really: the brown cat's-eye glasses framing soulful brown eyes, their faintly hyperthyroid bulge making them appear to brim with tears; the zipped mouth as if it's taking every ounce of strength for her to maintain her dignity. You better keep your mouth shut, the mother says to herself; if you don't, all will be lost. He still loves you, she adds, though no one would ever know it from his behavior, and she feels a sudden shoot of tenderness poke its way through the wet black dirt of her heart, which she just as suddenly yanks up to study: the unformed bulb at its base, the fragile hairlike roots. Why let tenderness get a purchase when it can only serve to weaken her position? But *you're* the one who won't allow it, she says, waving her spatula at the window.

She's wearing a white blouse with a peter pan collar, tucked into a pair of madras-plaid bermudas. She has a nice figure, the mother, but the older daughter thinks it would be a fate worse than death to end up saddled with such generous breasts. Better far the wild and disembodied soul navigating the trackless waste! The ghost hand scrabbling at the windowpane. Better far to be a ghost outside a house looking in, especially at night when the lights are on and you catch glimpses of the people you loved when you were alive going about their business. Though how you'll ever find the house in the first place, your soul drifting among the pricked ears of the firs, specks of light above, specks of light below, stars or windows—it will be so difficult to tell them apart!

Up and down the rugless hallway Tiny Tears rides in her blue stroller, its right front wheel loose and squeaking on its axle. The younger daughter is wailing like a baby, pausing to sternly whisper (it isn't time to eat yet, Tiny), wailing again. In this family everything talks to itself, including the parakeet (hello pretty mommy cupcake) and the exhaust fan (mrrrt mrrrt murder murder), referring to its deadly internal duct where so many flies have met their end in a grease-clogged net of cobwebs.

Meanwhile the father is slowly approaching the back door, crossing the tiny lawn bordered on both sides by stockade fence (blocking out to the left the O'Rourkes' jumble of toys, laundry, and unmowed grass; to the right a garage, and Terry Caruso's shiny black Cadillac), and at the rear by the white-washed retaining wall up which red roses climb to the foot of a huge willow marking the edge of the Dodge dealer's lot, the entire neighborhood having been built in terraced steps along a steep hillside. Could it be the summer of 1955? The willow fell during a hurricane, filling the yard with its limbs, crushing roses, smashing windows with its green fists.

Though why cleave slavishly to historic fact: there are fissures and tunnels and trapdoors (cobwebbed ducts too) in the brain, the watery tracts and coral castles through which the little shining seahorse floats—now you see it, now you don't!—and despite a prevailing sense (at least among those who don't believe in an afterlife) that being remembered is the closest we can get to immortality, the simple truth is that it's not just in our memory where the dead reside.

For instance as I watch my father approach the back door there's something spare and almost ascetic about him, though in most photographs from that pre-hurricane period his face shows the sort of plump, pretty-boy quality my grandmother took for a sign of weak character, whereas it probably only meant he liked to eat. My mother is frying a meat-cake for him and it smells good.

Nose, nose hairs, breathe in, breathe out ... An invented character never *really* dies.

The exertion of digging and planting, combined with an increasing heavy moistness in the air, a hot gusty wind from the east possibly filled with rain, maybe even thunder and lightning and hail, has made his dark hair curl, has brightened his cheeks. He too wears a white shirt, one of Henny's expertly ironed shirts that he'd normally save for the office, except this one has a frayed collar, and the stain on its front placket is becoming more and more visible the closer he gets to the house. The phone rings on the little chest squeezed between the refrigerator and the swinging door to the dining room, its drawers containing things rarely or never used (owner's manuals for such

broken appliances as the deep-fat fryer whose cord likewise lies
hidden deep under a pile of ruffled aprons, a lemon zester, a
muddler, a croque-monsieur mold, a set of pastel plastic heart-,
spade-, diamond-, and club-shaped cookie cutters, a bartender's
guide called *Here's How* bound by rawhide thongs to a pair of
hinged wooden covers, etc. etc.). The phone rings again and I
look up, annoyed, pry apart two of the blind slats and peer out.
A cloud must be passing over the sun, for the yard has darkened.
I too can see my father from my window, picking his way
around the wrought-iron furniture on the fieldstone patio he
built during the year after my birth. The yard is his domain:
sometimes very late at night I notice him sitting there in a
wrought-iron chair at the far end near the birdbath, staring back
at the house in his white pajamas, highball in hand, dachshund
on lap, his face illuminated by one of the blazing lights strung
at intervals around the Dodge dealership.

No, I hadn't heard, my mother's saying into the phone,
just as the door opens and closes and the first drops of rain are
tossed against the window as if in a spirit of merriment, a few
landing on the patio, black speckles on a gray field. A second
handful, a third, then nothing. My father sneaks up behind her
and ... what? Gooses her? That was just Terry, she says, swat-
ting at his hand. Once upon a time they'd have embraced with
fervor, scorned the prevailing idea that desire such as theirs
couldn't ensure marital bliss. The prick of Cupid's dart, a
wound you can't let heal but must keep picking at.

They're predicting gale force winds, she says.

Who is?

Are. Terry heard it at the store. Do you want me to slice an
onion? We should check the Sterno.

But who says? He gathers his plate, grabs a beer from the refrigerator, and heads for the dining room, where the sound of cheering soon emerges from the radio, an overwrought male voice. Robin Roberts on first. Nothing about a storm, though the rain has started up again, this time in earnest. It's streaming down the two windows looking across the driveway and into the Carusos' well-lit dining room, where young Joey can be seen drinking a glass of milk, old Joe and Terry, Cokes. The hippocampus (seahorse of smell and memory) releases from its pouch a school of odors: salt on cast-iron, seared meat, burned fat, pepper, rain on dirt, the almond smell of Jergens on my mother's fingers.

In my room I sigh, stretch, readjust the pillow against the footboard, yank loose the yellow quilt from the foot of the bed, and climb under, facing the window. I'm so drowsy. Water's running into the bathroom sink. Now it is time for your bath, Tiny. The room is getting darker and darker, the rain hitting the roof with a sound like little rubber-shod hooves, the sound you hear right before you faint. From the kitchen the click-click-click of the dachshund's toenails on the linoleum; my parents' voices a distant burr. Not drowsy, no. Sad, rather: "Be with me always—take any form—drive me mad!" Nothing saves you from the grave, Cathy Earnshaw, and should passion call you back, well then, watch out ...

... FOR I WAS A GIRL NOT QUITE AS OTHER GIRLS
are, my delight not dependent on playing nurse to a brood of
empty-headed dolls nor on reading the minds of my energetic
chums, no, even as a girl I preferred to take for a companion an
egg, a potato, a capon, a nut, to replace the dulling rainfalls of
human intercourse with the fiery windstorms of the kitchen,
my original guide in this endeavor Antonin Carême's *L'Art de la
cuisine*, wherein I soon enough uncovered, in rapt perusal of
those fragile pages, those intricate plates showing gâteaux in the
shape of Greek temples, galantines like nests of eels, those infinitely branching trees of information (see FORCEMEAT, see
ISINGLASS, see SOLE), the contours of my true nature, for Edwina Moss was, Gentle Reader, that most solitary and haunted
of creatures, not unlike yourself, willing to forsake family and
friends, to ruin my health, to conceal myself for all eternity in
an ever-deepening cave of cooking implements even late into
the bliss of a summer night, still faintly sensible to the muffled
voices of my parents, to the antiphonal music wrung from the
hind legs of insects, to the combined smells of pine-tar soap
and decaying rose petals and pipe tobacco, to the heat of an
oven almost too warm to be tolerable, and yet, AND YET!
deep within my cave I might feel stirring the apple-scented
breezes of a Norman bourdelot, the fishy winds of a Corsican

stew, the almost skunkish fumes of the Périgordian truffle, for such is the sleight-of-hand accomplished by even the most mal-adroit of cooks who, like an illusionist's dove, will continue to exist in the here-and-now while at the same time having utterly, ecstatically, vanished ...

SOMETHING IS WRONG IN THE HOUSE.

Something has been, is, and always will be wrong in the house, though at first glance you'd never guess.

The mother is in the kitchen, the Parcheesi "man" she sometimes uses as a potato masher clamped under her arm since her fingers won't bend. On the white stove a copper frying pan and in it three split peas; on the white kitchen table three slightly-smaller-than-tabletop-sized pewter plates, a plaster milk bottle, a plastic ketchup bottle, a Venetian blown-glass tumbler (the only one left from the original set of six). In the dining room the father is propped so stiffly in his chair that his eyes are trained on the ceiling, even though there's a newspaper waiting to be read on the table, its single headline (HAZEL HITS PHILLY! EVERYONE DEAD!) eye-catching to say the least. One daughter is taking a bath fully clad (her red-and-yellow-checked dress sewed to her torso) with her thumbnail-sized porcelain dolly. The other is in the rosebud-papered night nursery, lying in her trundle bed reading as per usual, the book's deep blue cover (black twisted tree, yellow moon, yellow-and-black clouds) glued to a single disappointing block of wood.

And then just when you think it will go on like this for-ever there's a flicker of orange in the upstairs bathroom. Some-body falls off the edge of the world and lands far far below in what might be mistaken for a boat of some kind but is really a fur-trimmed moccasin. Momentarily everything is so bright it's as if color and dimension no longer exist; there's a loud crack, followed by a plunge into eerie midday darkness.

The living room sofa (minus cushion) is on the second-floor balcony, the father in the broom closet, the broom and dustpan on the coffee table, the gilt-framed mirror in the third-floor bathroom, the dog-in-a-basket on the roof between the two chimneys. There is a giant soup spoon on the floor, its bowl face up in the hall blocking the door to the broom closet, its stem extending through the doorway and into the living room. It's easily twice the size of the girl who is lying on the floor right next to it; no one seems to know how or when it got there. In the yellow-tiled kitchen the butler is reaching his handless arm toward the mother lying spread-eagled atop the table.

The storm has come on so fast no one is prepared; the lights go out.

Sergeant-Major Morris is at the door with you-know-what in his pocket ...

Stop it you're scaring me.

Baby.

I'm telling.

Yeah sure.

Another flash, another crack but louder, different, the sound of something actually being torn asunder. The phone rings, an antic fraction of a ring, meaning it's the storm calling. The storm hopes you'll pick up the phone so it can zap you through the wires.

Girls! Girls! Your mother wants you in the cellar.

In the basement we can barely stand to look at one an-other. The Sterno stove has been hauled out of the carton where, normally, it is stored with other emergency items: the bedpan, the salmon poacher, the vaporizer. And while there isn't any fuel, there are plenty of canned goods, though chiefly the ones no one wanted upstairs (Campbell's Scotch Broth, for instance, which Henny claims smells like human sweat). No chairs either and the floor's too damp to sit on. Maybe this is the first time we've all been in the basement together: usually we come separately, my father to hammer or saw, my mother to hang laundry, my sister to play dolls, the dachshund to pee in the corner behind the laundry sink when the weather is inclement.

The whole house shakes. The giant picks it up and shakes it. This is a family given to the idea of apocalypse, some of us because we know we deserve to be punished, others because it suggests a convenient way out. .

JUNE 23, 1982. EDWIN D. WAKES FROM uneasy dreams to find a pool of water on the floor beside his bed, a gentle rain pattering in, all that's left of last night's storm. Though he has a distinct memory of jumping up at some point to close the window, it's still wide open, the curtains dangling there like a pair of arms, waterlogged and limp. Of course it's always possible he got distracted. Who wouldn't? There was a lightning ball caught in the yard, bounding from stockade fence to rose trellis to brick wall. The dachshund whined, the heavens opened. The world was restored to its primal condition, his Dodge to a giant teardrop sliding away on a river of tar, his heart to a crystal of salt. Then again, maybe he left the window open to bug Dorothy.

The room is so dim and gray, the bed so soft and warm, the dachshund's sleep so enviable, that he's having difficulty staying awake. Once more the rain seems to be falling harder, foiling his every attempt to identify sounds, the oddly liquid tumble of something in the wall behind his head, the bang of metal on metal in the kitchen, a distant crepitation in the backyard. Footsteps scurry down the hall toward the door where they pause, then continue even more rapidly, stopping at the head of the stairs. Henny? Please let it be Henny! But Henny's dead, and besides, who can afford a cleaning lady these days? The girls haven't lived here for years. It could be Dorothy, but isn't she in the kitchen, slamming stove lids around like an insane drummer?

At least he can count on the dog to stay put, snoring noisily in his usual place next to the heat vent at the foot of the closet. Good old Noodle III, the last in an illustrious line of family dachshunds, guarding the stockpile of liquor bottles from his thirsty mistress, who's been known to jimmy the lock. It won't hurt to close our eyes a little longer, right, fella? Two can play at this game. Back in the old days, before the oldest daughter moved out of the room and he moved in, the closet was full of those lank funereal garments she favored. He tries rolling onto his side, but finds it impossible to imagine what message his brain might send his limbs to get them moving.

There's no avoiding the fact: something happened during the night. The windows seem both farther away and larger, the light fixture and the maple dresser to have disappeared. There's a smell of flowers, unfamiliar and sweet; flies buzzing and not a swatter in sight. Maybe he's got motive mixed up with emotion. Certainly he's never felt so lonely, despite the presence of whoever it is monkeying around out there in the hall. The grandfather clock is striking the hour, reminding him that he's supposed to be somewhere, that he's supposed to be doing something somewhere in a manner consistent with his role as head of household. But when he tries to raise himself on his elbows, forget it.

Here boy. Here. Luckily a dog's snore is essentially companionable, without the human snore's smug standoffishness. Through the noise of the rain he can faintly hear a sucking sound, like hooves in mud, the jingling of a curb chain, the squeal of saddle leather. When he was a boy in Foxchase he used to cut quite the figure on horseback, clearing the fences with inches to spare while the girls applauded, knockouts all of them in their summer dresses ... But it's time to get up. Time to rise and shine, as Dorothy likes to say. Time and tide wait for no man. So full of sayings, Dorothy. A regular fashion plate herself before she took to buying slacks from the Haband catalogue.

He tries to recall her face and is distressed, then amused, to discover that he can't, just as he finds it amusing that his notorious appetite suddenly seems satisfied by the mere *idea* of food. Evidently the molecules of his brain have undergone total rearrangement, their previous system of cause and effect replaced by a complex pattern of cells (dishes?) deployed against a white ground, felicitous yet shifty, contributing to his dawning sense that if he doesn't get busy soon, all will be lost.

It's still raining, the pool on the floor rippling in a weak breeze. Little by little he becomes aware of what sounds like a parade on Germantown Avenue, a brass band marching past the cut-rate pharmacy where the car lot used to be. They're playing "The Battle Hymn of the Republic," one of his favorites, though to the best of his admittedly screwed up recollection Memorial Day's over, the Fourth of July still to come. Ba-boom ba-boom-ba-boom-boom-boom the coming of the Lord. He is driving down the highway in a pink and yellow Ford. A loud noise to the left of his head underscores the song's insistent rhythm: whoever's in the hall seems to be banging urgently and heavily on the bedroom door, their fist falling at regular intervals in time with the music.

Hello? Hello? Are you alright? An irritating voice, one he vaguely recognizes. His eldest's taste in friends wasn't always so hot. Keeyooshun, he replies. Keep your shirt on. I know you're in there, the voice whines and all at once it comes back to him. Little Joy Harbison, of course! He'd recognize that whine any-

where. Meanwhile Noodle has awakened and is sniffing frantically along the crack at the foot of the door when it bangs open,
disgorging a shapeless girl, a pitiful excuse for a hat rammed
over her yellow cloud of hair. Poor little kid, he thinks. Something happened to her years ago though he can't quite remember what, only that it was bad. I found *this* on the landing, the
girl announces, clutching a large doll in both hands, holding it
out for closer inspection. Almost as if someone threw her down
the stairs, she adds darkly.

The horses are impatiently stamping their hooves, the
band playing louder now. Obviously a crowd has gathered on
the sidewalk, singing along and waving flags. The littlest children will have woven red-white-and-blue streamers through the
spokes of their bikes. There's no use crying, the girl says. What's
done is done. She pushes the doll closer, removing the head to
show him where it snapped off at the neck. Though it ought to
be obvious it's not the doll that's making him cry but the memory of Dorothy standing at the foot of the driveway, squinting
through the viewfinder of the Brownie 127 as the girls coast toward her on their bestreamered bikes. It should be glued
RIGHT AWAY before your daughter sees it, the girl says.
Benny gave it to her, I hope you know. You can cry later. Also, in
case you haven't noticed, your dog needs to go out.

He can't stop staring at the little white neck, at the way it
imploringly curves toward the place where its head used to be.
What does it want? What the hell does it want? Regular glue
won't work with porcelain, but there should be a tube of Duco
cement in the basement, in the upper left-hand drawer of the
Mother Goose nightstand where he also keeps the Elmer's, the
LePages, and the putrid stuff made from horse hooves, and
where the girls used to keep their Ginny doll outfits.

Once something breaks it's impossible to restore it to its original condition, though this observation would also seem to hold true for any kind of change, the constant movement of furniture within a house for instance, the nightstand's gradual fall from favor, from girlish sunny bedroom into dark abyss. Maybe this explains why he feels like the room he's in doesn't really exist. Or possibly existed once years and years ago, back when it was inhabited by his daughter, a small child but getting bigger every minute, the logical result of all that roast beef he worked so hard to bring into the house.

The yellow-haired girl is standing beside the bed, crooning loudly (don't worry, honey, Mr. D. will fix you, you just wait, you'll be better than ever and no one will want to throw you down the stairs again or take off your wig to tease you), though her display of maternal concern is so clearly an act it makes him want to laugh. And just how do you happen to know about the wig, Miss Smartypants? Huh? He makes another effort to lift himself, to grab the doll and see whether it's as he remembers—the open bowl of the head, the eyes waving on their little stalks like a lobster's, the wig lost and his daughter inconsolable—but only succeeds in dumping his blankets on the floor.

RRGTHH! he yells. Dorothy! If just for once she'd get up off her duff when he needs her. The rain thunders, the music swells. The girl tucks the doll under her elbow like a loaf of bread and begins tugging his arm. She's surprisingly strong, though no match for him, for the great heap of flesh he's become. Come *on*, she says through clenched teeth, bracing her knees against the edge of the bed. Come *on*! She screws her eyes shut, takes a deep breath, and then all at once he feels himself moving, jarred free like the stone from the mouth of the tomb in the illustrated Bible his mother gave him for confirmation, the image so vividly printed on his mind that he makes one wild attempt to look over his shoulder at what's been let loose before he lands with a crash on the floor.

Under the bed great tumbleweeds of fluff and dust slowly revolve. He can see a black sock near the wall, and beneath the maple nightstand a coupon of some kind. Mary Kitchen? Mrs. Paul? Of course, that's it! Today is double coupon day and he was planning to drive to the Acme to do the week's grocery shopping. He can hear the sound of applause, the band striking up again, closer than before, almost as if it's marched right into the backyard. Watch out for the flowers! Watch out for the hose! There's a muffled scream, and then an angry voice—bad dog! bad dog!—followed by a scuffle, the squealing of hinges, a burst of noisy weeping, a slammed door, silence. How peaceful and warm it is down here on the floor. You could almost fall asleep, if it weren't for the smell of melting glue, like smoke pouring from the knacker's chimney.

SOONER OR LATER THE HOUSE WILL GET the best of you. It will defy your attempts at narrative because it's opposed to content; it only honors form. The basement, for instance (where we found ourselves imprisoned, hiding from the hurricane)—the basement's usually empty. It doesn't become a hiding place until people are hiding in it. Otherwise it's a hole at the bottom of a house. The things it contains (furnace, soapstone sink, workbench and tools, shelves and boxes, garment bags, pipes and ductwork, clothespins, canned goods, mice) are without inherent drama, even though one of us has wept over the sink, another has wrung out in it her blood-stained underthings, another has fed raw meat and lettuce to the box turtle briefly living there, rescued by my father from certain death on the Blackhorse Pike, that romantically named stretch of highway he drove each day to work. In the turtle's eye a prick of light, though who knows if its source is the bulb over the workbench, ricocheting first off the shining jars filled with screws, nails, bolts, washers, nuts, springs, etc., or something less tangible. Folded around mothballs in a steamer trunk my grandmother's opera cape, the nipple-colored negligee my mother wore on her honeymoon, misshapen baby clothes, little handknit garments frighteningly stained with excrement or rust. Garments as briefly inhabited by me or my sister as the

sink was by the turtle, the negligee by my mother, and cata-
logued in *Our Baby's First Seven Years* along with the name of the
knitter: pink silk sack (Caterina Zara), white knit rompers
(Marie-Thé-Lambert), yellow booties (Mrs. A. Dinger), pink
booties (Eleanor O'Gorman), matinee jacket (Millie McCree).

Of course every house in the world, no matter how well-
built, will eventually catch fire, blow up, wash away, get knocked
down to make way for something new. No matter how durable
a house, it isn't immortal. Whereas there's always the possibility
that there was more to Caterina Zara than what's suggested by a
pink silk sack. For this reason the house is jealous of spirit and,
as is often the case, becomes possessive. This is why houses are
haunted and why, if you love the form of a thing too much,
there's really only one way out.

T HE *EVENING BULLETIN* SAYS SHE WAS wearing a red playsuit, my grandmother remarks over dinner at Henri's, despite my grandfather's attempts to shush her. He was always so much nicer. Here, he says, handing me the menu to hide behind. Rasher of Bacon, Shad Roe, Rollmops of Herring, Sweetbreads. In the night nursery this is what Miss Mouse feeds the dolls when they've been naughty. Meez Mausse— French, like my grandmother. Pudding for dessert, though it's made of plaster and won't quiver. Alma, Herodotus, Roly-Poly. We don't eat what other families eat; our food is perverse. Puddings small as grains of millet, puddings big as mountains. Nesselrode, Flummery, Blancmange ...

Foul play, my grandmother predicts, raising a finger of melba toast to her querulous rosebud mouth; the shad, she tells the waiter, but only if it's very fresh. They're saying accident, my father corrects, pointing for the waiter's benefit toward the lobster tank, ignoring my mother's narrowed brows. (The expense, she's hinting. Don't expect my father to put on your plate what you can't afford on *your* puny salary.) It's as if we hold not menus but playing cards.

Haltertop and shorts! Exposed midriff! My grandmother raises one eyebrow, sips her manhattan. What could the child's mother have been thinking? The lobsters wave their antennae, open and shut their claws. Both Harbisons are doctors, but *she's* the neurotic one, my mother explains, then turns to the waiter. Caahve's liver, she pronounces, like a Noël Coward heroine. The waiter hovers, pen poised; he knows on which side this family's bread is buttered. And will it be the usual for Monsieur? But my grandfather is looking at me with concern, nervously clacking his dentures. Pink, my mother adds. Stop clacking, Daddy. You're not going to faint again, are you, sweetheart?

As if anyone ever does so on purpose—unless of course it's your only means of escape from an impossible situation, trapped with a perverse family in a dark brown restaurant, wreathed in cigar smoke, the waiters creeping behind you with their trays of horrifying food, peas in blood, fish eggs in filmy sacs. The real reason not to wear a red playsuit (or order lobster) is because, as Edwina Moss wrote in that darkest and brownest of centuries, the gods prefer their food red … though under certain circumstances they'll try anything, the heap of bone and gristle Prometheus foisted off on them. So you might imagine them sitting around Olympus like Brillat-Savarin's gourmands, "eating slowly and savouring every morsel, the movement of their jaws smooth and gentle; each bite having its special accent; and if they happen to pass their tongues along their gleaming lips …"

There she goes again, says my father. A regular Camille. The next thing I know I'm on my back and the gods are looking down at me with dubious, you might say gleeful, concern.

O! there can be no species of slaughter so inhuman as when under the plea of making the flesh white, the calf is bled day by day, a sharp pointed knife run through the neck severing all the large veins and arteries up to the vertebrae, the skin taken off to the knee and to the head, which is removed, the carcass opened and dressed, kept apart by stretchers, and the thin membrane, the caul, extended over the organs, the heart, the liver ...

Cause of death? It's never simple. For instance does Beth March die of scarlet fever, or is she the victim of her own goodness, her unselfishness, the fact that she tends the sick Hummel baby when none of the other Little Women can be bothered? Goodness won't protect you; if you're too good you will die, but then it can be seen as a kind of reward. Both Little Diamond, who dies of goodness and fever, and the Little Prince, who dies of goodness and snakebite, have longed to "go home" to heaven. When the Little Match Girl freezes to death on New Year's Eve it is her only means of joining her dead grandmother.

You'll die if you're too little, but also if you're too loving, especially if, like Anne Shirley's beloved Matthew Cuthbert, the object of your love requires your death to learn an important lesson or advance the plot ("... and no life is ever quite the same again when once that cold, sanctifying touch has been laid upon it"). For this reason parents are frequently expendable: Mary Lennox's mother and father die of cholera in India ("... the place was so quiet ... no one in the bungalow but herself and the little rustling snake"); Elnora Comstock's father drowns in the Limberlost ("... that oozy green hole with the thick scum broke, and two or three big bubbles slowly rising that were the breath of his body"). The deaths of animals, unless anthropomorphized (e.g. Charlotte) don't count, ditto supernatural deaths (anything in Poe; the son in "The Monkey's Paw"), though Cathy Earnshaw's an exception, since knowing whether she dies of madness, consumption, or a broken heart ("... nothing that God or Satan could inflict would have parted us, *you*, of your own will did it … I have not broken your heart—*you* have broken it; and in breaking it, you have broken mine") is crucial to measuring her future power as a ghost.

So it can happen that an ounce of prevention will turn out not to be worth a pound of cure. Nursed at a mother's breast and raised out-of-doors in sunshine and clean air, three meals a day of wholesome food, plenty of milk, fresh water? No matter. The public towel is a scourge, likewise public swimming pools, a kiss, a breath. Vaccinations will not help, nor screens on your windows, pounce-boxes, lightning rods, an aligned spinal column, a pure heart, an unblemished soul.

We waited out the storm in the basement. It smelled worse than usual, oppressive, airless, with undertones of sulphur, mildew, bleach. What light came through the two small cobwebbed windows, one facing the street, the other the backyard, was a strange blackish green. Is that Gold? my father asked, stationed at the front window, though how could he see anything, the webs, the dim light, the rain lashing the pane? There was a snarling sound; my sister, who'd been trying to put the dachshund in the salmon poacher, began to cry. If you don't tease him he won't hurt you, my mother said.

My father was referring to Benny Gold, who lived directly across the street, his house an exact mirror image of our own, save for the flatness of the front walk, its three steps as opposed to our fourteen, and the presence of rowans (which according to cabala protect against demons, being without thorns and inedible) on either side of his stoop. When Benny Gold opened his door you could just barely see into a room where, in place of our piecrust table, there was a strange honey-colored chest decorated with sinister black knobs and spindles, and on it a white lamp-shade atop a glass globe filled with what looked like India relish.

Though it wasn't until you were all the way in that the mirror's defects really struck you. For in our house, where my mother'd hung the Manet print of the masked harlequin I thought was the Lone Ranger, Benny Gold had hung a ram's horn and a brass sextant. In the bow window recess, instead of the camelback sofa where my mother's friends sat smoking and drinking sherry when I came home from school, he'd posi-tioned a complicated hi-fi system and a bust of Socrates among inviting heaps of books, dirty laundry, and LPs, mostly jazz. Framed by an archway in our house, the gleaming mahogany table Henny polished every Tuesday after sitting at it to eat her solitary egg salad sandwich; likewise framed, Benny's Formica table, where it was impossible to eat your marshmallow fluff sandwich until he'd cleared a little space. And while we too had bookshelves—built into the wall behind the piecrust table and filled with Heritage Society books (not one but two lavishly produced *Rubiyat*s for instance, the edition of *Candide* my little sister adored with the illustration of a woman whose buttocks were being sliced like roast beef)—the shelves in Benny Gold's house didn't match and were everywhere, books spilling onto the floor, stacked here and there, paperbacks with lurid covers, red Oxford University, green Bollingen, peeling cellophane *Livre de Poche* … Camooooo! Benny coached us. Say Camoooooo!

Like the angel of death, the hurricane's eye was passing overhead. The small parlor of Lakesnam Villa, blinds drawn, a fire burning brightly. "Hark at the wind!" says Mr. White, who is about to welcome his old friend Sergeant-Major Morris into his house, not knowing that he has the monkey's paw in his pocket.

They should've let it burn, I remembered Polly Keck saying—sitting with her chin resting on her knees, her tan arms prettily cradling her tan legs—and Joy Harbison replying, of course they *should've*, but why? If there's heaven, who'd want to come back? And if there isn't, it's not like a *paw* could change things.

At the time we were all crowded together in the oppressively airless Hermit Cave (Benny and his whole adoring entourage), and he had just finished reading us "The Monkey's Paw," one of those heartbreaking tales about a man who's granted three wishes, but because he fails to imagine every possible loophole, ends up with less than he had to start. A *paw*, Joy repeated, and I remembered Benny looking at her in a way that most adults, who were thrown off by her dull expression and little yellow eyes, didn't. Not admiration, you understand. Oh no, never admiration. At the time I thought Joy, who seemed to make a virtue out of dullness, couldn't have cared less. Weren't you listening? Benny asked. The paw had a spell put on it by a fakir. He wanted to show that fate ruled peoples' lives and that those who interfered did so to their everlasting sorrow.

Benny Gold. He was a skinny man with infrequently washed, unfashionably long dark hair and hornrims, a man completely unlike the other men on our street who emerged from their front doors at the same time every morning, their minds rehearsing scenes of commercial conquest, and returned at the same time every evening, loosening their ties, dreaming of cocktails. Benny Gold on the other hand seemed to come and go as he pleased: like a seabird he might stalk off at midnight on his long stiff legs, whistling, a duffel bag slung over one shoulder, and return at dawn two months later. Bachelor and intellectual, sailor and Jew—Benny Gold was a romantic figure who regularly starred in whatever delicate gentile daydreams the respectable women of Boxwood Road, my mother being no exception, would permit themselves from time to time. Of course the fathers hated him. Care for a nut? he said to me, holding out a little cellophane bag as we stood side by side in Caruso's Market, watching Mr. Caruso expertly grind beef.

The hurricane's eye passed over us. The willow fell. It broke the kitchen window and the storm's noise came inside.

This is it! my mother screamed. This is it! But then she was always braced for the worst, hers the stance that wards off blows, leaving to my father the role of assailant or repairman. You could hear things hitting the linoleum floor, things rolling, breaking: glass shards, garlic heads and buttons, the million pieces of the cachepot my father planned to glue together when he got a chance. After his stroke I found them heaped on the bottom shelf of the same cupboard Joy tore apart, together with an unbroken Quimper bud vase. Guess whose? he'd asked angrily, but we all knew it was part of the set Marie-Thé-Lambert was bringing my mother, item by item, from France. More often than not this is the ruling condition of adult life: your anger at what breaks turns to anger at what remains intact.

It's him alright, my father said. The damn fool's out there in a yellow slicker. Put the dog down, honey.

Noodle loves me, my sister said, he wouldn't ...

Camooooooo. I am on the third step and I want your liver. Which would you pick? The lady? Or the tiger? Benny Gold, endlessly instructive, like most autodidacts. But what was he doing outdoors in a hurricane? "A cold wind rushed up the staircase, and a long loud wail of disappointment and misery from his wife gave him courage to run down to her side, and then to the gate beyond. The street lamp flickering opposite shone on a quiet and deserted road ..."

THE WISE MAN BUILDS HIS HOUSE ON rock, the fool on sand, and truly there is no more important factor than location in your choice of dwelling place. The direction in which the house faces, for example, whether alone on a hill overlooking a rain-dimpled pond in a long deep valley, or among other houses and barking dogs in the valley itself; whether exposed to the cold gusts of the north wind or to the cool scrutiny of neighbors; whether high or low, lurking in shadow or plain as day—all of these features will determine the quality of the life lived within the house, just as the soul of the cosmopolite is shaped by his body's contact with his fellow man, the soul of the anchorite by contact with everything but. Do not make fish of one and flesh of another. All feet tread not in one shoe.

Houses facing south are warmer, but subject to greater changes of temperature; those facing north are cooler, their temperature less mutable. Houses situated in dark forests or between dense clumps of trees are apt to be damp and unwholesome, though a woods at some remove can be an advantage, furnishing oxygen in abundance. It is best not to live near a factory, a mine, or a hospital, for even the sweetest spring breeze can be the carrier of injurious gases, vapors, germs. Swamps and marshes likewise make bad neighbors, though their pernicious effect can be vitiated by plantings of eucalyptus in the tropics, sunflowers in more temperate zones.

Of course you'll have nothing to say on this score, scripture failing to address the subject of where the wise woman builds her house. The giant sunflower's message is haughtiness; the dwarf's, O! I adore thee.

However careful we are in the situation of our homes, may we not be made ill in other ways? Do you think, if you could, you would always be well?

THE MOTHER, MEANWHILE, HECTICALLY pushing her carpet sweeper back and forth over the same square inch of blue carpet sample, has come upon the father, spread-eagled on the floor next to the plaster milk bottle. This is what happens, she says, when you don't love me enough. She gives him a little poke with the sweeper, then sighs and continues cleaning the carpet, its shade of blue identical to his eyes.

It's more painful to do nothing than something, the father says. I ought to know, Dorothy, I've been lying here for years. Oh, she doesn't realize it yet but she's a hilarious sight, cut right down the middle like a pie.

And still the mother keeps pushing the sweeper, not so much incapable of sympathy as distracted from the father's plight by the pile of kibble she's just discovered behind the larger of the two sofas, the one with all four legs and no cushions. Mice, she pronounces, and the father nods. Maybe if they had a cat instead of a dachshund? Or if the dachshund hadn't eaten the turtle, since a turtle in your cellar has a smell known to repel mice and rats.

In any case the mother's right, for here comes a mouse now, scurrying across the green wooden "lawn" and into the living room, where it freezes, nose atwitch. Eeek! A real moose looks like Bullwinkle, but a real mouse looks nothing like

Mickey: those wet little eyes, those needle-bright teeth, that stunningly three-dimensional body quivering with life. If you think what you're doing *now* is nothing, says the mouse, just you wait. *Now* your brain tunnels are still open, but soon they'll all be clogged, even the left hemisphere. Then it'll be nothing doing, literally. Even a brainiac like that kid of yours, the mouse says, darting its wet pin eyes toward the ceiling. One of these days, nothing doing. Even my babies, their little heads cracked open like walnuts. Of course that's the risk, living with animals.

The mother thinks with sudden tenderness of her own brain, perilously riding in its basin like a sultan in a howdah. Lucky for me I don't have a heart, she says, bending the wire stem of her neck, bringing her head closer to the father's. Only wires and fluff, she adds.

You aren't listening, says the mouse. We're talking about him.

Unlike the mother and the mouse, the father's practically impossible to see. Only when you close your eyes can you picture him perfectly: the expression of cunning on his handsome face as he contemplates his situation disturbed from time to time by dim flickers of fear. The mother may not have a heart, he laughs to himself, but at least *she* has a mouth, whereas the hole in his head he once swallowed into and spoke from has grown bigger and bigger until it's all that's left of him. Meanwhile his voice is getting smaller and smaller; you have to shut up the house to keep even the smallest particle of what's left from leaking away, the least smell, the cool odor of his skin, vanilla and urine and talc. A horrible thing to die, he says. Like that little girl. It's pitiful. They should have locked Gold up and thrown away the key. I could go for a cup of coffee right about now, by the way. Nice and hot, not like this junk, he adds, pointing to the "milk."

But that was ages ago, the mother reminds him. The willow, the window. Why are you going on about it? How angry she looks, since it's just occurred to her that the father might be getting ready to leave her behind forever in a cloud of dust. And Joy Harbison wasn't exactly what I'd call petite, she concludes morosely.

The shadow cast by the mouse covers the entire room, because it's a living mouse and a monster. Forget coffee, it tells the father. I said "nothing doing," weren't you listening? You aren't allowed to handle boiling water anymore. As for coffee, you're permitted a hot beverage but only if you can trick someone else into making it. Leave out your cup, and if you're lucky your wife will take the hint.

She'll dump it down the drain, the father says. I know her. Then he sighs. I wasn't always like this, he says. I wasn't always so out of it and limp. It's the food they give you here, green beans and noodles and worms. Poor old Noodle, we didn't bury him deep enough if you ask me.

The father sounds annoyed, weary, and the mother knows that if she doesn't catch on soon, he'll go away, leaving her to spend the rest of her life with a mouse. Noodle? she says.

The very one, he replies. He's back here every night by the light of the moon.

Though another way of putting this might be: in my father's house there were many mansions and they were all the same, labyrinthian interiors smelling of damp plaster and varnish, the dark hallways narrow, hung with sepia prints of places no one ever visited or would ever dream of visiting—Hong Kong, Abu Simbel, Nasirabad—a seemingly endless bolt of oriental carpet streaming down the stairs and flooding the rooms, its disconcerting flotsam bobbing up in isolated squares of sunlight, all those grimacing flowers, horned faces, toothless mouths flung to the nethermost nook and cranny, lapping here against a broom closet door, pooling there around an umbrella stand, puddling at last beneath a snarl of hair and dust.

Well-appointed, of course. On the cherry chest a brass lamp, its silk shade fringed with pink tassels impossible not to braid into pigtails while the grown-ups drank their cocktails and the radiator knocked. (My grandparents' parlor, 135 Locust Lane.) In the glass-paned bookcase *Twice-told Tales*, *De Rerum Natura*, *Kim*, *Fragmente der Vorsokratiker*, *The Bedside Book of Famous British Stories* ("The Adventure of the Speckled Band," "The Apparition of Mrs. Veal," "The Man Who Would Be King," "The Monkey's Paw," etc., etc.), *L'Art de la cuisine au dix-neuvième siècle*, *The Little Lame Prince*, this last covered in green morocco, its frontispiece showing the blackly cross-hatched ceiling of Hopeless Tower, and the

crippled boy—or possibly not crippled but perched atop an ele-
phant, or possibly not a boy but Lucretius or Carême—rising on
his cloak above the hundred-mullioned, barrel-vaulted window
casement in the tower wall to bat his head over and over against
the hundred-mullioned skylight like a trapped fly. (Benny Gold's
living room, 26 Boxwood Road.) Red-and-white-checked contact paper covering the shelves upon which are arranged Staffordshire teapots, tinned copper saucepans, cross toasters, mustard
pots, pewter candlesticks, fine-meshed sieves, bottled plums,
beeswax candles, chafing dishes, Dutch ovens, tortoise-shaped
tureens, castellated pudding basins, Venetian blown-glass tum-
blers, brass weights, measuring cups, knives. (Joy Harbison's
pantry at Ashgrove, intersection of Boxwood and Bellevue
Drive.) A beakless parrot on a parrot stand. A porcelain child
bound by wires for all eternity to a tricycle of blue lead. A one-
handed butler. (My mother's dollhouse.)

The dollhouse is made of wood painted white, its facade
swinging out like a door to reveal the rooms of the two lower stories, its red gabled roof hinged at the peak and opening upward
to reveal the attic. It's very old. It first belonged to my grandmother, who gave it to my mother, who in turn gave it to me. I
used to keep the dollhouse on the maple dresser in my bedroom
with the I LIKE IKE and MADLY FOR ADLAI decals pasted to
the top drawer, twin symbols of my parents' fundamental dis-
cord. One Christmas, against my mother's objections, my father
added electricity; he affixed a tiny bulb to the ceiling of each of
the six rooms, and hid the wiring under adhesive tape.

Open, the dollhouse remains a toy; it's impossible to ignore the improbable presence in it of big fingers, their crass ability to put the toilet in the living room, the butler on the roof.

Better by far to keep it closed, to wait until dark and plug it in, to peer through the windows and inspect the mother (upright, thank God!) as she stands in the kitchen dully regarding the lid from one of those clear plastic containers toothbrushes come in, piled high with molding barley. A treat for my Gertie! she thinks, for she is capable of thought so long as the dollhouse remains closed. So long as the dollhouse remains closed it's possible to believe its contents might prove infinite, that the kitchen might actually give onto a shadowy pantry where a tiny mother (not the frowsy-haired doll but a real woman with blood running through her thread-thin veins and nimble fingers the size of eyelashes) is selecting from among a vast array of implements a pudding basin like a pasha's turban, a sheet of isinglass, a handful of bitter almonds. Outside the house, a wind-rippled pond. A real pond, not a mirror.

But there is something wrong with the daughter; she has no interest in food. And O! how difficult it is for her mother to find her. There are so many rooms in the house, and they are endlessly mutating, shifting position: the miniature cedar chest at the foot of the miniature trundle bed no longer filled with minute bed linens but with thick woolen blankets, its now heavy lid lifting to release the cedar's sharp medicinal smell into a large, tall-ceilinged room papered with rosebuds, a four-poster mahogany bed opposite a Queen Anne highboy, in the top middle drawer of which is hidden not a tangle of long kid gloves and a jet evening bag with a red lip-shaped stain on its white satin lining, but a small porcelain head, nor is it a passing car's headlights that make the drawer pulls shine, but a pale northern sun turning a pine floor the color of honey, and out the window black spruce, a thawing pond, the sound of a train whistle, a trolley car, Mrs. Caruso starting up her Cadillac.

The daughter is waiting for her mother; that's the way it is when you're sick. You are either waiting for someone to arrive, or waiting for someone to leave. This is because no human being can ever begin to compete with your illness; it's all yours, unlike people, who come and go.

Through the doorless kitchen wall (briefly disturbing its molecular integrity) and into the dining room, around the claw-foot table (molded lead painted to look like oak), and through the back wall, carefully negotiating a webwork of dusty wires, and down a long dark hallway lined with glass-paned bookcases (Shakespeare and Plutarch, spiders and flies, purple heart in a purple velvet box, *Encyclopedia Britannica*, Louisa May Alcott, E. T. A. Hoffmann, conch shell, dyed egg in a robin's nest), and into the parlor, setting the lamp tassels astir, the barley likewise solidifying into one of those puddings the Victorians called Shapes, a tremulous castle emerging from a brown Staffordshire basin and borne aloft past the deer antler coat rack, the silver card tray, and up the stairs, flight after flight after flight, the sound of water dripping from the eaves, the millrace swollen, and then the sun's first little finger points at its own face in the grandfather clock on the landing, the clock strikes six (a whole sleepless night of Westminster chimes waxing and waning as if to mock the body's relentless downhill course) and the mother arrives at last in the bedroom where her daughter lies exhausted on her maple bed, afflicted as it will turn out with a dramatic nineteenth-century disease (though the doctor's initial scornful diagnosis was "high-strung") ...

My mother handed me a Quimper bowl, the hand-painted Frenchwoman in the bottom covered by a watery layer of junket. Downstairs the refrigerator door was opening and closing: out came the Hellmann's, the celery, the egg. For some reason I didn't understand, Henny was never allowed to make her own lunch, as if she were a guest instead of a cleaning lady. I could hear the sound of chopping through the heat vent, my father saying something in a low teasing tone and Henny's burst of laughter. He can't help himself, said my mother. As long as it's in a skirt ... Needless to say, back then women didn't wear pants. In my mind I could see Henny clear as crystal, sitting there at our dining room table in the faded brown-and-white-checked dress she wore for cleaning, a wiry and erect little black woman, chewing and swallowing egg salad, dabbing mayonnaise from her mouth with one of the "good" paper napkins. I could see her grizzled hair, as close to the scalp and curly as Tiny Tears's—Henny always removed her plaid kerchief before beginning to eat.

Downstairs sandwiches were being eaten; the sun was charging in through every newly washed window. Downstairs the world was moving toward the future, while up here my mother was fiddling with the venetian blind cord, drenching the bed in darkness. By the same token, my father was saying to Henny, you can't beat Glass Wax. Dreamily, almost aimlessly, my mother began to recite:

> I remember I remember the house where I was born
> The little window where the sun came peeping in
> at morn
> It never came a wink too soon nor da da da da day
> But now I often wish that sun had borne my breath
> away ...

... AND YET WITH WHAT CUNNING DEVICES THE world conspires to erode the cook's painstakingly erected walls, to insinuate through their every chink and gap its seductive airs and breezes, to pose, in short, so surreptitious a threat to one's belief that it might at last (at LONG LONG last) be possible to leave behind forever mother and father and sister, the whole history of a life reduced to the faint memory of a poem learned in childhood, a single line of it recalled intact, the rest having dropped first into isolated phrases—*little window, wink too soon, borne my breath*—then into single words—*sun, morn, away*—then into no phrases, no words, only a persistent wearying pulse—*you are no one, no one at all, height without mass, motion without motive*—that when at last I idly plucked from the tower of books at my elbow *L'Art de la cuisine*, when at last arrived that fateful day on which the great Antonin Carême himself undertook my corruption, the portrait he presented of himself as both genius ("I have created an infinite number of new things!") and lost soul ("I have tortured myself in body and spirit by wakeful nights!"), as well as the manner in which his gaze met mine, in which it confronted me from out of the etched frontispiece— wary, languid, with those gently sloping shoulders, those full lips which suggest, depending upon the beholder's disposition, either frank sensuality or the sepulchral worm—so thoroughly out-Heroded my Herod, I was the more aroused, the less vexed, readily conceding him master of that selfsame role to the perfection of which I'd heretofore devoted all my lonely hours, eagerly making my way to the kitchen only to falter, to freeze, to stand there dumbly waiting—for inspiration was slow to strike, Carême kept me diabolically as if it were part of his plot to nurture my discomposure, an effect he'd have known would be enhanced both by the room's location in the very bowels of the house and by its furnishings, the fact that such space as was taken up in other rooms with familiar sofas, chests, lamps, was here occupied by shelves on which were arranged a variety of strange apparati, equipment sinister to the uninitiated eye, all looming over a solitary table, its knife-gashed surface somehow managing to give at once a sense of the pileous and the slick— if, for all that, I met my subsequent failure, the dismal aspect of my first attempt at a pudding, with mute acceptance, if I ended by nursing the sorry illusion that at least Carême had deigned to honor our tryst, albeit like a reluctant suitor, offering no apology for his lateness, his behavior instead providing every indication that he took himself to be alone, yawning, scratching, his preliminary neglect as disconcerting as his air, so constant at this stage, that my every word, my every gesture, represented a point of departure, the paradise imperative to all journeys ...

Has it stopped raining? Or is it just that the bedroom, only moments earlier lively with the sound of slamming doors and band music, now seems utterly still? There's a white porcelain head resting in a pool of water right under the window, scraps of cloud, a buzzing fly. The clock is chiming, though it's impossible to tell *which* half hour without looking at it. Ding a ding dong, etc. etc. So why not get up? The sleeping fox catches no chickens. Why lie on the floor when there are millions of chores waiting to be done?

The head, for starters, needs gluing. Isinglass dissolved in gin would be ideal, if it weren't for the fact that Guess Who drank all the gin. Besides, the isinglass tin is empty now, the house gray and damp. The girls shouldn't be outdoors in this weather, especially the eldest with her lousy respiratory system. No one should be outdoors. But then no one should be left alone on the floor, either.

Of course in this house loneliness is never a very private matter. For instance the dog still seems to be sniffing along the crack at the foot of the bedroom door, from the other side this time, in the hall. And someone's downstairs in the kitchen, drawing a knife through the sharpener screwed to the wall just above the potato bin. Over and over, the sound broadcast by the heat vent, *voosh voosh voosh*, energetic but careless, letting the filings fall onto the potatoes. The doorbell is ringing, too, possibly the mailman. Or maybe the doctor, because clearly there's a problem here, one arm so heavy—a giant's arm!—it won't move at all, while the other ... Oh, the other's a beaut alright, smooth and white, not unlike the aptly named Nora Devine's arms, but much too delicate to prop the torso, let alone grab hold of a bedpost and pull the whole giant body to a standing position.

Still, it might be possible to creep toward the window, which seems to have retreated farther away than ever, but after all, the journey of a thousand miles begins with a single step. Good arm, good leg, good arm, good leg. Elbow, knee, elbow, knee. The floorboards widening, the gaps between them like mileage markers on a lonesome highway, the car limping along with two flat tires, nothing but dust as far as the eye can see. And then just when it's beginning to seem hopeless, there's the electric outlet with its two cords, one white and one brown, leading to the maple dresser, then disappearing behind the dresser and emerging on top, where they connect, respectively, to the plastic alarm clock and the brass lamp with its hand-painted picture of Valley Green Inn, a pair of horseback riders, a sliver of creek specked with ducks. Hundreds of ducks, quacking, scooting with amazing speed over Coke-colored water as the girls toss them bread crusts. Noodle I straining on his leash. A typical family outing in the good old days, back when getting from one side of the room to the other was no big deal.

But isn't this how it started in the first place? One minute you were feeling sorry for yourself, stuck in an unhappy marriage, and the next thing you knew you were lying on the floor, hungry and shivering and completely alone, feeling sorry for everyone. And the lonelier you felt, the more monstrous you be-

came. You wanted to fly in the face of the gods like the monster
in that story of Dorothy's, risking punishment just to improve
the lot of creatures no bigger than your fingers, dressing them
up and feeding them, moving them from room to room, dis-
pensing advice ... Vinegar and oil, rubbed in with flannel, and
the furniture rubbed with a clean duster, provide a very fine polish. A great many homes stand without strings like the frame of
a harp, suggesting music in form and outline though no melody
rises from the empty spaces.

Meanwhile here at long last is the window, taller than remembered and therefore closer to the floor, making it possible
to plant the good elbow on the sill and slowly lever the torso
into position. Not unlike jacking up a disabled car, the Dodge
having come to a halt on the sandy shoulder of the Blackhorse
Pike, and Nora Devine blowing smoke rings from her dark red
lips, watching amused from under a billboard where a huge pair
of dark red lips is blowing smoke rings. Spike heels of her pink
sandals sinking bit by bit into pink sand; white smoke rings
emerging one by one from her dark red lips. Puff puff puff. Way
to go, loverboy.

Puff puff puff—you can say that again. Though at least it
seems to be turning into a nice day, the sun breaking through
the clouds and the sky a light shade of blue. The Carusos are in
their backyard, drinking beer and barbecuing. Porterhouse
steak no doubt, thick and pink, the fat sizzling on the coals, the
juices trapped inside. Some people have all the luck. Some people have their own private meat locker. But that's the way it
works, isn't it? The smell of grilled steak goes up your nose, and
the next thing you know, your mouth is green with envy. Even
the gods must feel it, doomed to eat ambrosia and nectar when
there are smells like this rising from below.

And really, when you think about it, how much better our world is, seen from above and through a window! The breeze so fresh and the garden coming along nicely, marigolds and zinnias and stringbeans, yellow birds chirping in the dogwood. Everything perfectly formed yet miniature, right down to the people in their colorful outfits far far below—suddenly the people seem most enviable of all, even if faintly menacing, those little mouths full of teeth and ready to speak. Daddy! says one of them. But she's a grown woman with a daughter of her own, so what's she doing in a long old-fashioned dress, standing there with Henny in the middle of the crowd, both waving flags?

They're spellbound, every last one of them, listening to a man in a blue uniform deliver a speech, seated on a large gray horse. He's barely visible within the thicket of flags and fancy bonnets, raising both arms like he thinks he's the Pope, his horse lowering its goosy neck to nibble the tender seedlings. Benny Gold, natch. The beans are being destroyed, but Gold's too busy talking to notice. The time is nigh blah blah blah our moral obligation blah blah . . .

As might be expected after a heavy rain, the lawn's teeming with worms, and the little yellow birds are swooping down in great numbers to yank them loose. Noodle, too, way back at the foot of the rose trellis, is digging away like mad, though it's not worms he's after. No, Noodle's after the truth, which would be abundantly obvious to everyone if they weren't so busy listening to Gold. If they weren't hanging on Gold's every word they'd see that the second a bird has removed a worm there're ten to take its place, and then ten more, fifty, a hundred, a thousand. More worms than you can shake a stick at, the whole yard crawling with worms, and that's because the soil can't hold them, because in the beginning (which everyone's conveniently forgotten), before there was a 27 Boxwood Road, before there was even a goddamn road, the builder reduced his costs by injecting the bedrock with softener so that now it can't hold anything.

THE TOWN OF X IS SITUATED ON THE same longitudinal axis that extends north through the ice-choked waters of Baffin Bay, home to walruses and seals, then up across the frozen waste of Ellesmere Island and into the Arctic Ocean; southward it traverses the quaking Chilean coast, the ver-glased peak of Mount Fitzroy, vanishing at last under the treach-erous waves off the tip end of Patagonia. To the east, the heaving swells of the Atlantic, sunny Barcelona, the blinding Gobi Desert, mountainous Hokkaido—all the way across the vast blue Pacific to what has by now become the west, Seal Rock in Oregon, Cloud Peak in Wyoming, the Great Lakes, and back again to X. Thus you might imagine the town firmly strapped in place by those endless invisible lines, like the point on a package where it's necessary to press the string down with your finger be-fore making the crucial, final knot.

Of course you'll probably object that such an image is misleading, positioning irrelevant X at the center of things. You'll object, that is, until you remember that no matter how diligent your attempt to accept the idea of citizenship in a world where the boundaries separating Barcelona, Fitzroy, Cloud Peak, Baffin Bay, are mere inventions, you know it's a joke, and that where *you* are is dead center, the target's seductive heart. Narcissism and paranoia have always gone hand in hand.

Which no doubt explains the persistent belief among X's inhabitants that long before the first settlers appeared in 1780, long before the first mill was built (and with it the foundation of a thriving lumber industry), there was an even earlier mill, maybe not a true mill at all, but a demonic engine designed by the *genius loci* as a plaything for his simple-minded daughter. According to proponents of this belief, the original mill wheel was made from the bole of a tree so immense that before it was felled it cast its shadow across the entire valley, turning whatever grew there squat and colorless. You can still find vestiges of that vegetation everywhere you look: pearly shoots of broom-rape and Indian pipe scattered through the town's forests; fleshy knobs of mushrooms, veils of fungus in its cellar holes.

Just as each spring you can still find slivers of the wheel heaved up out of pastures and front yards. Cunningly carved all from one piece, each of its vanes thin to the point of transparency while at the same time impossibly strong, it was mounted on an iron shaft where a raised sluiceway could channel tons of falling water onto it. The water set the vanes in motion, the shaft rotated, the complex system of gears inside the mill began to spin. The great stones turned. Whirring and scraping, clacking and grinding: *skree-skraw, snurre-rur, kribble-krabble, cranch-crunch.* It was dark in the mill, dark and moist, water beading and dripping down the walls, along the pitted metal of the gearworks as the daughter frantically adjusted the flow, into the hoppers and down the chutes to the stones. Water to vanes to shaft to gears to stones—the tumult was overwhelming! Every so often shafts of light broke through like imploring maternal fingers, but their plea for moderation went unnoticed.

.   .   .

Of course any sound you're forced to listen to, day in, day out, is bound to become at last inaudible. The town record begins where the story of the mill ends; history takes over with its passion for isolated squeaks and crashes, as if there were no X (or Y or Z for that matter, all those taverns and shops and churches and schools and cemeteries) until the first settlers arrived on the scene.

Arden and Jacob Starkweather, where on earth did they think they were going? *Away?* Could it be they were driven by nothing more than a need to escape? But then who can explain why such clearly archetypal journeys—twin brothers venturing forth *per una selva oscura*, where the unconscious spreads its great dark web, where the villainous agents of our fate lurk side by side with the magical agents of its reversal—should result in disappointment? Who can explain why such journeys always end with the forest dismantled, with nothing left except stumps and sawdust and that blinding light without which history (meaning all sense of destination, of the future) is impossible?

The previous winter's snow had finally melted, but each step Arden and Jacob took across the sodden forest floor threatened to suck the boots off their feet. How steep the hillsides, threaded with streams of wildly running water, thundering waterfalls, small quiet pools where the blackflies bred! The brothers' faces were pocked and raw, red welts crusting over with dried blood and the flies' dead bodies; there were flies in their ears, in their nostrils, in their mouths, in their eyes. Black spruce everywhere, unlike in Edwina Moss's day, when it'd all be chopped down to render the hillsides hospitable to sheep. Indeed the landscape was so uniformly dense with trees, so without boundary, that the brothers might have kept walking forever had they not found themselves at the edge of a cliff, staring down on the recently thawed surface of as-yet unnamed Egg Pond which was, in Jacob's words, "boiling with fish."

As good a place as any, they decided. While Jacob sat on a nearby rock, recording the event in his sketchbook, Arden began hacking away at everything in sight. The smell of sap and newly cut wood, of leaf mold and snails. Because the first tree had nowhere to fall, it leaned above the brothers at a precarious angle, caught creaking and groaning in the arms of surrounding trees like a giantess with the vapors. Black spruce, *Picea mariana*—it is said an advancing flora moves forward most rapidly in the habitats best suited to itself. Human migrations follow the same principle: to the victor belong the spoils; the loser must be content with what is left. Thus Jacob's charcoal sketch chooses to show Arden's face lit from above, by the weak light trickling onto it as if down the shaft of a well. "Arden Felles a Tree," the sketch is entitled, though the impression it conveys is not of a man hard at work, but of a man in the throes of sexual passion, vaguely debauched, self-absorbed.

Of course we have no way of gauging the artist's ability to remain objective beyond the evidence of his other existing work: a notebook filled with curiously anthropomorphic renderings of flowers (the sullen "faces" on a clump of red trillium or the horrified frozen "stare" of a birdfoot violet); a series of ink drawings chronicling the settlement's development (typically precise, cross-hatched); and Jacob's masterpieces, two large works in oil entitled "Heaven" and "Hell" that originally hung in the vestibule of the town hall on either side of a stuffed polar bear.

Both paintings show the millrace viewed from above, a broad horizontal swath of water like a loosened braid of shimmering translucent hair, bordered top and bottom with rocks, with a densely tangled net of willows, the entire scene in both cases brilliantly illumined by the sun. Summertime, the deep blue of gentians along the banks, silvery hints of fish in the water, the vermilion wing-patches of red-winged blackbirds flashing in the willows, salamanders shooting like bright arrows among the ferns.

But which is "Heaven" and which is "Hell"? At first glance the difference between the two paintings seems obvious enough—why, then, should it prove so impossible to describe? Is it that the predominantly sepia underpainting contains traces of cerulean in "Heaven," of terre verte in "Hell"? Is there a more complex system of glazes in the former, a heavier reliance on scumbling techniques in the latter?

Maybe the only way to tell the paintings apart is to admit that looking at them makes you feel like two separate people. For example, if you find yourself drawn to "Hell," it isn't merely due to the human preference for the funhouse over the swanboat. No, what draws you to "Hell" is the way it makes you see for the first time how your own eyes have been accented with pinpricks of zinc-white light, how around each and every hair on your head there hangs a faintly glowing nimbus, how each threadlike nerve, each radiant brain cell, each spinning atom, each quickening idea, is endlessly fascinating. Looking at "Hell" you look at your undeniable complexity and you think, so exquisitely have I been fashioned, there's no reason I shouldn't live forever. Whereas looking at "Heaven" all you see is limitation. Even the fish are prettier than you.

Arden felled one tree, two trees, three, four; Jacob kept sketching. The arrangement struck neither brother as unfair, though they both knew that even if it did there was no way out.

This was the lesson of Castor and Pollux. You were either a god and lonely, or mortal and beloved. The western sky turned rose madder, a great yawning mouth down the darkening throat of which the sun plunged. A far-off noise of jinglebells: the spring peepers singing and mating. Something large, heavy-footed, crashing through the woods to the east. Jake? Jake, you there? You ain't dead, are you? A sigh; the crackling of tinder. Arden was building a fire.

Nor did it occur to Jacob to include in his sketch the activity of the ants, the little stars clicking into place, the neck of the goose being cracked in two by a fox, the bloodroot flowers wrapped in their leaves like mummies. No, what he was really recording was the jealous throbbing of his own dull heart. What he was really recording was his urge to pluck out his own heart and replace it with his brother's. Kindhearted Arden, his deep gray eyes gazing into the fire, his voice absently raised in song. *O tell me tell me Tam Lin* ... He'd impaled a trout on a stick and was roasting it over the flames, turning it this way and that, the skin blackening, the fins and tail flaking away as char. *At last they'll turn me in your arms into the burning gleed* ... The sweet smell of cooked trout flesh, of juices dripping through cracks in burnt skin. Jacob's mouth watered; he shivered; he was filled with hate.

Any violent impulse, if not immediately acted upon, will burrow like seed into the ground, biding its time until the day finally comes, as the day surely will, when it will be allowed to bear fruit. The brothers didn't know it, but as they sat eating their fish beneath the great unfurling W of Cassiopeia, they were sitting in the exact spot where that first immense tree used to stand, where Edwina Moss, having put the finishing touches on *The Blancmange*, would strike the fatal match. The earth is riddled with such places. Edwina Starkweather Moss, great-grand-daughter of Jacob, *not* Arden; of the artist, not the woodcutter. A key distinction, since it's no secret that artists often are like the bad fairy in Tam Lin, that frightening ballad Arden used to great effect when courting the ladies. You alone can save me from my fate—such is the message of Tam Lin. You alone can prevent the bad fairy from stealing my deep gray eyes and replacing them with eyes made of wood. Marry me. Cast your green kirtle over me and keep me frae the rain.

ONLY IT DIDN'T RAIN. AFTER THE STORM it stopped raining; it became dry, too dry. Dust on the roses, the Cadillac, the rowans. No funeral to speak of, no "ashes to ashes dust to dust," because if your parents are atheists they'll pack your organs in jars like Egyptians and donate them to science, scandalizing the neighborhood. You could smell the asphalt heating up in the driveway between our house and the Carusos', softening, melting. ("All the way to Boxwood Road," as my father prophesied after his stoke, "the whole business sliding down, the grass and the skin and the driveway, no way to stop it, and only the earthworms to mourn.") Everywhere the smell of bitumen, that healing substance medieval apothecaries sold as "mummy," combined with the faintest trace of bleach, dirt, marigolds. There was a disturbance in the house, a scrabbling sound, a rustling, maybe fingernails on glass, tinder catching. Whereas in *Little Women* "the spring days came and went, the sky grew clearer, the earth greener, the flowers were up fair and early, and the birds came back in time to say goodbye to Beth, who, like a tired but trustful child, clung to the hands that had led her all her life, as Mother and Father guided her tenderly through the Valley of the Shadow and up to God."

All night long the #23 trolley, the palest of greens like a harmless little snake, hissed its way up Germantown Avenue, down Germantown Avenue. Brightly lit though mostly empty, except for the drunk tipping the twisted bag to his mouth, the occasional shopper, nun, cleaning lady. Not so many women knew how to drive back then. Jamie O'Rourke practicing to be a musical comedy star in the mirror on the other side of our medicine cabinet, his eyes the same piercing blue as the eyecup on the top shelf. Some enjanted eefning, Jamie would sing (not half bad, insofar as you could hear him), you vill fint a strain-cher … According to my mother, Jamie O'Rourke, whose father died in Korea, suffered from being raised in a family of women. My father was more blunt. The kid's a fairy, he said, shaking his head, unable to imagine a fate that to a ladies' man like himself was worse than death.

Semidetached—when you think about the fifties, that's a pretty good description of the entire decade. All the houses on our street were thus paired, not unlike (with a few notable exceptions) the people who bought them, charmed by the prospect of raising children in such close proximity to the truly la-di-da neighborhood right there on the other side of Germantown Avenue. In those days the families were young—the mothers and fathers younger than I am now—and the cement of the sidewalks was still new and white; pieces of mica would sparkle under your feet when you walked along, breaking or sparing your mother's back, depending on your mood. At night possums would lift the lids on the trash cans with their exquisite fingers.

According to Benny Gold, in the place of our houses there'd once been a vast meadowland extending from Germantown Avenue, where the trolleys spat electricity into the night sky, to the Wissahickon, where we used to go on hikes before Joy Harbison's body was found in a penstock the day after the storm. Paleo-Indians used to come here looking for mastodons, Benny Gold said, which they toppled like condemned buildings. Life was so much better then. He had nothing but contempt for agriculture. Some nights from the Club Milano on the corner came the sound of accordion music, bursts of laughter, people having fun.

Meanwhile I lay sleepless, the Westminster chimes waxing, waning, as did the sound of adult snores, the dachshund's toenails crossing the linoleum *click click click*, followed by a noisy wet lapping, metal tags clanking against ceramic, a wrenched gagging noise ... The usual sequence, though it seemed anything but familiar, just as the facelike light fixture on my ceiling suddenly reverted to its original and terrifyingly unfamiliar condition of pure fixture, the "eyes" and "mouth" to three silver balls attached to three silver chains, the "nose" to a translucent cone filled with dead flies.

What you want is always out of reach when you can't sleep. You can only have what you don't want, or what you thought you wanted, lurching toward you, unspeakable horror. The small parlor of Lakesnam Villa, blinds drawn, a fire burning brightly. "For God's sake don't let it in!" says Mr. White as the mangled body of his dead son lurches closer and closer. Joy's wide-set yellow eyes, her furze-like ledge of bangs, her slightly moist flaccid skin, unpleasing to the touch like a petunia petal ...

Oh there's nothing empty about insomnia; it's full to bursting! Chains of thought, some minuscule, tinnily chime in your pricked ear; some immense, wind Laocoön-like around your twitching limbs. You think you're waiting but you're not: you're awaited, though not by sleep. Insomnia is the wish to be immortal, granted by an ass. And should you make the mistake of seeking comfort from your mother, touching her gently on the shoulder and interrupting the rhythm of her snores, she will sit bolt upright, her eyes darker, more protuberant than ever without their glasses. What is it? she will ask, breathless with fear. Go back to bed, she will say wearily, once she has recognized you. It's late.

So you find yourself yet again in the long dark hallway. The night-light broken and thick with dust yet still inserted in the outlet at the head of the stairs. Possibly the saddest place in the whole house, though why, who can say? I am on the first step, as Joy liked to whisper in a deep voice, and I want your liver . . .

Joy Harbison, Joy Harbison. She makes my blood run cold, my mother used to boast, miming a shiver. And, truly, there was nothing charming or lovable about Joy, her squat body in its navy-blue school uniform, her little yellow eyes, her pale face that made you think of the surface of a pond, though not a lightly rippled summer pond with a suggestion of hidden depths, of thoughts darting among its deepest folds, but a pond in the heart of winter, a white disk of ice coated with snow, solid through and through. Nor is it likely that I ever would have had anything to do with her if it hadn't been for Benny Gold, since she attended private school and was the only child of well-to-do doctors, one plain, the other an astro-physician. They lived on the far side of a depressing triangle of dead grass that some people called a park at the lower end of our street, in a large mutton-colored Victorian mansion that actually had a name, Ashgrove, and was presided over by Joy's nanny, an exhausted and sorrowful Scottish woman named Miss MacConchie. Later when my mother took to drinking her solitary drinks from a bag-wrapped bottle in that selfsame park, it was Miss MacConchie who'd call my father to rat on her.

Takes one to know one, my father would say, hanging up. The window open over the sink, and a sweet little breeze blowing through the screen. Let's say he'd just planted several flats of zinnias. Then he'd kick the bottom drawer of the chest behind the swinging door (extension cords, clothespins, screwdrivers, skewers, cheesecloth, rubber gloves, nail polish remover, plastic Ginny doll shoes) and say to the dog, Well I guess I'd better go see what our girlfriend's up to now . . .

Sometimes my mother would be lying there sprawled on her back like any common bum. Shoots of new grass poking through the fibrous mat of dead vegetation. Lying there in the spring coat I watched her try on at Wanamakers, before we went to the Crystal Tea Room for bisque tortoni.

When you're a child you learn the rules for friendship from your mother and father. I was drawn to solitary Joy Harbison because she attached herself to me, just as I was drawn to Benny Gold because he encouraged me to attach myself to him. And while it's also true that he invited into his entourage young Joey Caruso, as well as sophisticated Polly and violent Henry Keck, some retard from Our Mother of Consolation, the sleazy and stolid Quaker Teachout twins, glamorous Jamie O'Rourke, and my cute baby sister (not to mention Joy Harbison), for a while I devoted myself to becoming his special pet. In those days I hadn't figured out that the more exclusive someone's attachment to you, the more difficult to remove them without pain and damage to your own hide.

But you don't listen to warnings when you're a child. For instance if I remember Benny Gold's lecture about the dangers of ticks, it's because he delivered it the same day I met Joy Harbison. At the time I made no other connection between the two events, aside from the fact that my first sight of her filled me with a dread bordering on rapture.

As usual we were hiking along one of the Wissahickon's many trails, panting with the effort, our bodies weighed down with gurgling Army Surplus canteens, backpacks full of hot-dogs and marshmallows. Oh, they're there alright, Benny assured us, pointing to the huge stalks of water parsley lining the trail above the ruined mill, the black spot in the center of each foamy blossom a perfect hiding place. If a tick attached itself to you, you had to dig it out with a penknife or the head would travel through your bloodstream to your brain. Bang, piped in a girl I'd never seen before. You're dead!

After setting out from Valley Green, Joy and I had fallen behind the other hikers almost immediately, she because of her limply pigeon-toed way of walking, as if her shoelaces had come untied, and also because she was laggardly by nature, trying to see how far she could push your patience before you'd snap. My own reasons were less clear, though like many adolescent girls I tended to mask my hatred for my body with a display of languor, almost as if I could make it stop changing just by dragging my heels.

It was a hot day, restless with humid breezes, the smell of horseshit and leaf mold, wet stones and fish. The soggy clearing where the water parsley grew had been sizzling with bees, thick with birdsong, but such clearings were rare. Indeed the prevailing mood in the Wissahickon was one of enclosure, like a vast nineteenth-century household threaded not with trails but damp hallways, the gorge narrow, the creek deep brown, the trees mainly hemlock, their message *You will be my death.* It's not surprising Poe was attracted to the place. What about Jesus Christ our Lord? asked Patience Teachout, who'd found the

story of the paw, its dim view of resurrection, upsetting. He was
never dead, said Henry Keck. He was just holding his breath.
("'Let me in, let me in! ... I'm come home; I lost my way on the
moor!' ... and, finding it useless to shake the creature off, I
pulled its wrist on to the broken pane, and rubbed it to and fro
till the blood ran down and soaked the bedclothes; still it
wailed, 'Let me in!' ...")

So you might say that one day Joy Harbison was hidden in
a blossom, and the next she'd dropped into our house. Nor did
she require an invitation but, because she was essentially un-
governed (despite Miss MacConchie's vague efforts to establish
control), you never knew where she'd turn up next: eating a
Lorna Doone at the kitchen table, dumping the dachshund in
the wading pool, pounding nails in the cellar. Once my father,
after knocking loudly and receiving no answer, found her seated
primly on the toilet reading *Life*, her red shorts around her an-
kles. Shortly thereafter my mother came upon her in my bedroom, playing with the dollhouse. Your daughter is with Miss
Waterbath, Joy explained. But it's Friday, my mother replied (or
at least this is how she later reported the conversation). *So?* Joy
was trying to remove the parrot from the parrot stand, prying
up its claws with a nail file. The riding lesson's Thursday, my
mother said, her voice rising. Watch out you'll—STOP it! And
then, chagrined to have yelled vengefully at another woman's
child, my mother asked Joy if her mother knew where she was.
Unh-unh, Joy said. Look, there's a mouse turd in the toilet. Can
I spend the night?

Eventually it became routine: I'd fling open the door and
there would be Joy, sitting opposite my mother in my father's
wing chair, sometimes wearing her boiled wool overcoat and red
tam-o'-shanter, sometimes one of Miss MacConchie's shapeless

beige cardigans, her "overnight case" (a grocery bag held shut with a row of paperclips) hugged to her chest. Her school let out a half hour earlier than mine, but in any case she'd've had to sprint all the way, since it was beyond the railroad station. She'd be there with my mother and (usually) two other mothers, like fluffy bleached Mrs. O'Rourke leaning from one corner of the camelback sofa to extinguish her cigarette in a blue glass ashtray, and phocine Mrs. Keck reared up in the opposite corner, barking for a light. As the mothers chain-smoked and drank sherry (its smell so deeply lodged in the breakfront shelf where the twin decanters sat that the only way to get rid of it was to sell the thing, even though I knew it had been my mother's prize possession), Joy watched them like a hawk. Took you long enough, she said.

But of course the mothers were relieved to see me: Joy cramped their style. Like whey through cheesecloth the sun drained through the organdy curtains and across the bow windowsill, over the sofa hump and onto Mrs. O'Rourke's creamy arm as she brought a silver table lighter to Mrs. Keck's Kool. I think Joy made them feel petty, babyish, at a time when they wanted more than anything to appear every inch the young matron.

Funny Mrs. Waterbath never called, my mother said, and Joy snorted. Mrs. O'Rourke and Mrs. Keck exchanged a look; a line of smoke rose straight from the blue glass ashtray, momentarily wobbled, straightened itself, spread into a cloud near the ceiling, blurred, and vanished. Outdoors the slippery shuffling sound of a lawn mower, the smell of cut grass. Heads up! yelled young Joey Caruso to the outfield (meaning the Teachout twins); Muffin, shut up! yelled ancient Miss O'Rourke to her ancient cockapoo, barking at a chipmunk in the flowering plum. When the mothers shifted position on the couch, you could hear the strange rubbery noise their girdles made. Funny Mrs. Waterbath, said Joy, opening the silent butler and removing a little red ball. This is just the kind of thing to choke a child.

Later that night when we were alone in my bedroom, she asked if I wanted to see the hair in her armpit. Why's your mother afraid of those bitches? she asked. They're just squares. Did I want to hear the song Benny taught her? Lady of Spain I adore you. Pull down your pants I'll explore you.

Afraid of who? And what did she mean, Benny? (For the idea of such a song coming from the mouth of Benny Gold, who seemed if anything a bit of a prude, was highly unlikely.)

But Joy just shook her head and told me I owed her. I lied for you, she reminded me. Did he go into that stuff about the salamanders? Did he play the hula record? She rolled her yellow eyes dramatically, then reached into her paper bag and removed an immense green volume called the *Library of Health* that she claimed to have found in her mother's office. Listen to this, she said. "Large-boned people should marry those of small bones, beauty should marry homeliness, nervous people their opposites." Good news, huh? For me, anyway, in case you hadn't noticed. She held up a wrist, turned it from side to side critically as if examining a bracelet. Saxon blood, she explained. Benny's wrists are more like yours.

What hula? I told her I learned to dismount at a trot, and about the different bits. Snaffle. Curb. We cantered across the covered bridge. My seat was greatly improved.

You slay me, Daddy-o.

We *did*.

Sure, she said. And my name's Milton Berle. Besides, you don't smell like a horse. No offense but you usually do after Miss Waterbath. Did I tell you I did the name thing and it came out marriage, but only if I used Benjamin? If I used Benny it was friendship. You were hate, by the way. I don't want to depress you, that's just how it came out, both ways, Benjamin and Benny. Sorry. Joy sighed and rolled over, taking the blankets with her. His birthday's in February, same as mine, except sixteen years apart. You ever think about your parents doing it? Doesn't it make you want to puke? Then she let out a sigh, rolled back, and as effortlessly as she did everything (like falling off a log for instance, or a dam) she fell asleep.

So we lay there in our cumbersome adolescent bodies, two girls side by side in a maple bed, one wearing the white pajama top she filched from her father's dresser because it smelled like Old Spice, which is to say like my father, the other the unbecoming pair of lime-green babydoll pajamas Miss MacConchie chose just for her at babyish Lillian's Lilliputians. Two girls awash in tides of trolley light, car light, lying there on their backs under a yellow quilt, one staring wide-eyed as if through the ceiling and into that black hood filled with the clamor and heat of stars, the other sound asleep.

Two adolescent girls on a hot summer night—hardly the material of great literature, which tends to endow all male experience (that of those twin brothers who found themselves adrift so many years ago in the dark northern woods for instance) with universal radiance. Faithless sons, wars and typhoons, fields of blood, greed and knives: our literature's full of such stories. And yet suppose for an instant that it wasn't the complacent father but his bored daughter who was the Prime Mover; suppose that what came first wasn't an appetite for drama but the urge to awaken it. Mightn't we then permit a single summer in the lives of two bored girls to represent an essential stage in the history of the universe?

Joy suddenly sat bolt upright. What's that? she asked, banging her head (shit!) against the maple headboard, like a dummy suddenly given life and no clue how to use it. Shhh, she said. Hear that?

But how could anyone's ears be so keen as to pick up the faint sound she would later claim woke her? Even Germantown Avenue was unusually silent, no crescendoing hiss of a trolley, no school of sparks flung from its cable. Not even the faintest rumble of adult snores from the far end of the hall, nor wind to stir the pre-Hazel willow's droopy leafless tresses. No rabbit to nibble lettuce. There was no lettuce, it was too early for a garden. Besides, in those days my father only planted marigolds, zinnias, geraniums, petunias.

Typically mysterious, Joy arose, pulling me after her down the stairs, flight after flight after flight, past the ticking clock, the rosewood parrot stand and the (*good morning good morning good morning*) nocturnally loquacious parakeet, past Henny's coat draped on a deer antler, the dark dining room's sherry-saturated mahogany and into the kitchen's web of shadows and lights, the linoleum floor with its design of tan-and-brown worms as uneven and rough as the root-crossed paths of the Wissahickon, though it certainly felt smooth underfoot. Back there, Joy said. Shhh! I can't believe you didn't hear it. The next thing I knew she was rummaging in the chest beside the fridge, locating and extracting from its tangled nest of cords and cookie cutters (Here's how *what*?, holding up the hinged bar guide) the ice pick that fell into disfavor the day my mother got the Osterizer.

This should work, she said, then sat on the floor and began removing boxes from the bottom shelf of the cupboard built into the rear wall: Cream of Wheat, Quaker Oats, Wheatena—winter cereals, consigned to their inconvenient position

the previous spring, their surfaces dusty, their contents un-
doubtedly infested with bugs. It's back there, she replied, pointing. Whatever it is.

Light from the Dodge dealer's lot was coming through
the window over the sink, illuminating on the sill the hollow
garlic heads, the dying violets, two highball glasses in the sink
engraved with the noble heads of Labrador retrievers. Or
maybe it was moonlight. A full moon risen to the very top of a
sky without clouds, far far above the pricked ears of the firs.
Here's how you make highballs, I said. But I don't think she
heard me because now she was lying flat on her side on the floor,
stabbing the exposed section of wall inside the cabinet with the
pick, her eyes closed to protect them from a cloud of plaster
dust. I couldn't believe what she was doing, but of course she
was as good as parentless. Got a saw? she asked, holding out her
hand, wiggling her fingers. A knife'll do.

Of course adults couldn't stand her, that sense of having
the wind knocked out of them on impact. They didn't need her,
because when adults got bored they fixed themselves a drink.
Dry Sack, highball, manhattan, martini. Maybe Crema Danica
and saltines or Triscuits, or Vienna sausages on toothpicks
(stuck into special holes made for that express purpose in the
ceramic dachshund with a pretzel-holding wooden stick for a
tail). Lipton Onion Dip with chips. Shrimp cocktail on special
occasions. So what if the children were dying of starvation? The
good ones, which is to say the cowards, either perished or devel-
oped lively imaginations or made friends with the bad ones.

The knife sawed through the lath; Joy's pasty spatulate
fingers reached into the hole. I shuddered, drew a deep breath,
spied with my overstimulated eye on the shelf directly in front of
me what seemed to be a shining phalanx of bottles and jars ad-

vancing in the moonlight, Tabasco sauce, Worcestershire (Lea & Perrins, is there any other kind?), grenadine, bitters, orange marmalade, preserved ginger. Vanilla extract, almond, lemon, anise. Maraschino cherries, one jar without pits and stems, the other with. Pit in the fruit, fruit in the jar, jar on the shelf—the denser the web of details, the more impossible to escape, as in the interminable songs (I don't know why she swallowed the fly …) my father sang to drive my mother crazy, interminability being the sadist's favorite device. There was a smell like the one in my grandmother's bedroom, sweet, musty, then sharper, more acrid, as when you pulled open the drawers of her Queen Anne highboy, or peeked inside the laundry hamper. Shit! Joy said. She yanked her hand back and put it to her mouth. Shit shit shit.

At first, since my view was blocked by her lime-green back, and since our kitchen had been infested not all that long ago with what my mother insisted on calling "watah-bugs," I thought an insect had scurried from the hole and up her arm—a caramel-colored cockroach about two inches long, with delicate pincers and black sawtoothed legs—but that was before I saw the silver-dollar-sized drops of blood on the linoleum. Falling fast, almost soundless, blip blip blip.

What happened? I asked.

An accident, said Joy, irritably, in the tone of voice that would come back to haunt me—*an accident*—weeks later, when my mother tapped on my bedroom door and walked in to inform me with characteristic glee that she had "bad news." Interrupting midspeech (Let them eat cake!) the doll mother whose head had just fallen off. The butler dead in the bathtub. (À moi, ma chère amie!) Eventually everyone would be dead, rich and poor alike, paving the way for Napoleon and Josephine and the beautiful houselike cakes of M. Carême …

I cut myself, Joy added. Ta dah. She unfolded her fingers and showed me what resembled mouths, red lips opening to reveal pinkish white tissue, one set of small mouths across the bottom joints of her fingers, and one big mouth in the center of her palm. Two or three bloody razor blades (the old kind, sharp on both edges) lying on the empty shelf.

What happened? I asked again.

I think maybe you should wake your dad. Sometime before it snows, she added, since I wasn't moving, loath, I confess, to let him see the mess she'd made.

But by the time I'd managed to haul him back with me to the kitchen, Joy (a doctor's daughter, after all) had fashioned herself a tourniquet out of the muddler and one of my mother's decorative dish towels (Declaration of Independence, middle drawer under the ruffled aprons), wrapped her hand in another (Gettysburg Address), and was mopping the floor with a sponge. Let's have a look, my father said, standing there in his maroon bathrobe, his dark curls tousled, his long lashes beating charmingly against his plump ruddy cheeks. Until the last year of his life there was never anything even remotely ascetic about my father, his plumpness the pleasing attribute of a well-fed man, a man bursting with vitality, an ardent carnivore.

No, Joy said. Shouldn't you be dressed? Or do you want me to bleed to death?

It must have been three in the morning, in other words the middle of the night, and the emergency room waiting area at Chestnut Hill Hospital, though well-lit, seemed oddly dim, as if my eyes were failing, or as if to symbolize the power of darkness over light. A bell-toned dinging, like the elevator at Wanamakers. Dr. Frankenstein? Paging Dr. Frankenstein? My father's pajama bottoms were peeking below his trench coat, while for some reason when Miss MacConchie arrived she was wearing an emerald satin cocktail dress and smelled overwhelmingly of cigarette smoke.

The razor blades must have fallen through the hollow space between the O'Rourkes' house and our house, my father explained. Though since we both had the same peculiar slot in the back wall of the medicine cabinet specially designed for discarded blades, who could say whose blades they were? I knew he was trying to charm Miss MacConchie, but was getting nowhere fast.

People actually *use* those slots? she said, laughing thinly, as if at a really tasteless joke.

... AND WHY NOT ADMIT THAT YOU'RE SICK TO death of it, of each pathetic attempt to squeeze the past like a blanched nut from the present's papery skin and onto a waiting tongue, when what you really want to do is pry open the mouths of the dead, to admit ONCE AND FOR ALL that despite its elegant appointments, its pleasing proportions, its windows giving onto a garden where rain is beading on the roses and a dog is unearthing what looks like a lump of suet, the house you presently inhabit may not necessarily be the house where you live, though you'd never describe it in such terms, or at least not at first, preferring to say that you are uneasy, that you are experiencing dis-ease, which is to say, in *this* house, *now*, as if it's actually escaped your notice that when you superimpose houses one on another, dollhouse on semidetached, semidetached on cottage, gaps and cracks appear, places where the walls and doors and windowpanes and closets fail to line up, oddly flickering interstices that seem pitch-black and genuinely hollow (unlike in the human body where despite the heart's apt designation as a "hollow" organ there's not a single empty space to be found), and out of which you will hear (at first faintly, almost like the soft throat-clearing that precedes utterance, that warns a listener to pay attention, then grows increasingly loud, more insistent), a beloved voice well up, though where it's coming from who can say, for one minute it seems located in the attic, the next, the cellar, one minute at a supernal remove, a loose cog in the machinery of the spheres, the next minute near at hand, possibly even issuing from the laundry hamper, yet it scarcely matters since you can never actually hear the words, they refuse to be pinned down and everything is in constant fluctuation, the little yellow birds replaced by starlings, nor will that cloud hold still long enough to allow for accurate description despite its tendency to fling a handful of raindrops at the same spot, over and over, just beyond the dogwood, and as for the suet, it will prove on close inspection to be the head of a doll, its face smooth and snow-white, not unlike the lard sculptures with which Antonin Carême decorated Napoleon's table at Malmaison, whereas God worked with mud . . .

PHILADELPHIA, ST. JOHN'S EVE, 1982. The angel of death was on the prowl, his tread barely audible now that the whole house had wall-to-wall carpet, an impractical pale shade of fawn that showed every little stain. Unbearably hot as usual, the driveway melting, sliding into the street. My father was sleeping in the maple bed in my old bedroom under the white sheet I'd eventually find crumpled in the hamper and stained with shit and vomit. Or perhaps it wasn't the angel of death but his emissary, as my father later described him: Noodle III arisen from his grave in the backyard, uprooting in the process the giant allium just to the rear of the birdbath. He came to me, my father said, though this was after the stroke. Good old Noodle, drilled through by maggots.

The house was unbearably hot.

From where he lay my father would have been able to see the landing, light from the cut-rate pharmacy making its way through the slats of the bathroom's venetian blinds, striping the carpet, the laundry hamper, the grandfather clock. He'd have been able to see the thick layer of dust on the night-light at the head of the stairs. The bulb burned out years ago, so why not remove it, throw it away, wash the damn thing at the very least? Well? Well, Dorothy? Cat got your tongue? It was one of his last remaining pleasures, and one he shared with my mother, this knack for fanning aggravation into fury. Crud everywhere, and whatever became of the girl he married, whose zeal for housework once approached the fanatic level recommended by such nineteenth-century experts as Mrs. Beeton, Mrs. Childs, Mrs. Beecher; the girl whose daybooks so endlessly chronicled her obeisance to the household deities of order and cleanliness? Mend things for cleaners. Iron skirts. Take wash from basement. Exchange shoes and decanter. Clean hall closets. Cut out skirt and blouse. Send Helen's card. Sprinkle clothes. Aspic for Mother. Red Cross Meeting. Baked ham, baked beans, applesauce, cole slaw. Wash & Perm. Windows. Tomato preserves. Polish brass & silver. Snapper soup, lobster, green salad, hard rolls. Put woolens away. Take woolens out.

Mrs. Caruso said she heard yelling, though whether that was both of them before the stroke, or my father during or my mother after, we'll never know. In any event the yelling itself would have been clear enough, the windows open, it being so hot, and the distance between the two houses just a little more than a car width, specifically the width of the driveway plus a narrow strip of dirt along the wall of each house. Cases of apoplexy mostly occur in stout, strong, short-necked, bloated-faced people who are in the habit of living well, says Mrs. Beeton. It strikes like a thunderclap, a bolt from the blue, which is the Latin meaning of the word.

How many times had it been *my* body lying in that maple bed, *my* eyes staring sleepless into that grim portion of the upstairs hall? Overhearing from across the hot asphalt young Joey Caruso whistling popular tunes, "Secret Love," "Fever," "Green Door," the notes traveling to me on the hot air sweetly like birds? The difference was, my view had never been obscured by the little speckles and dots of light that precede a so-called cerebral accident. When a man is asleep, said Mrs. Moss, his pulse beats and his lungs play; he is without sense and can be easily awakened. When a woman faints, she too is without sense, but she has no pulse and does not breathe. Apoplexy is between the two: though the heart beats and the lungs play, you still can't shake the man back to life. If the clot be small the effect will be light; if it be large the effect will be grave, the sufferer losing consciousness as if felled by a heavy blow. The face will be flushed and the pupils of the eyes generally dilated, or one dilated and one contracted. Breathing will be slow and labored, snoring may occur, the cheeks puffing out with each respiration, the air being blown through the lips . . .

My mother had the presence of mind to call an ambulance, after which she seems to have done nothing. Edwina Moss would have told her to bleed her husband, apply leeches, shave his head, empty his bowels—anything, in short, to release an excess of humors.

It is unfit to eat, madam, says the butler. See for yourself: drilled through by maggots. He's the spitting image of Fred Astaire though nowhere near so lithe, and also highly flammable, being made of celluloid.

They're standing together in the yellow-tiled kitchen, the butler with his back to the mustard-colored tin icebox, his handless arm indicating the plastic cap full of moldy barley on the table, the mother towering over him, in her arms the plaster dog-cum-basket, not a pet but a burden, like the boulder Benny Gold told us Sisyphus rolled up the mountain over and over and over again (say it, he said, as we sat, winded, in a circle around him on the dirt floor of Hermit Cave, having borne our picnic supplies up a steep path to get there: Cam-oooo! Cammm-ooooo!). Mold! the mother screams. This is an outrage! Do you want to kill the child?

Sun pouring through the two bedroom windows, striking the maple dresser (I LIKE IKE! MADLY FOR ADLAI!), the Battenberg dresser scarf, the maple bed. Sun pouring in despite what sounds like a torrential downpour but is really Joey Caruso washing his mother's black Cadillac, the water making different noises depending on how far the hose is from the car: a loud metallic drumming, a steady plashing, a gentle drip drip drip. The trolley hisses its way up Germantown Avenue; the steam iron hisses in the kitchen where Henny is talking back to the radio. Ain't no such thing, she notes amiably, positioning a sleeve. Whiter than white. My father shoulders through the screen door, his arms filled with bags. (Sirloin wrapped in blood-soaked butcher paper, tankards of gin and rye.) Hot enough? he says. Time to knock off, you gorgeous thing you. Go on, Henny replies, playfully lifting the iron in his face so it hisses even louder.

In the night nursery, in her pink hospital bed (Tootsietoy, molded lead, c. 1920), red-haired Gertie (German, kid torso with porcelain bust and hands and feet, c. 18—?) clutches a gray plastic dachshund (MADE IN JAPAN) while she tosses and turns on her tufted satin mattress and pillow-tick bolster (both hand sewn for me by my grandmother, c. 1954). Her eyes are closed but she's not asleep. She can't sleep, given the overwhelming heat of the Philadelphia summer and the brilliant sunshine pouring through the wall-less side of her room, not to mention the fact that her crocheted dress is sewn to her torso and her shoes won't come off because they're painted on.

How many will you be for supper, Madam? asks the butler. He's doubled as cook ever since I overheard my grandmother remarking that she always chose Henri's over our house because the world's great chefs (Montagne, Escoffier, the divine Carême) were not only men, but French. We will be thirteen, says the mother. No, make that twelve. Thirteen at table is bad luck. (The tone brisk, imperious, in frank imitation of my grandmother, whose firmly held opinion this is as well.)

Little by little the twentieth-century smell of wet asphalt, paste wax, and spray starch is supplanted by the nineteenth-century smell of varnished wood, mildewed books, and damp wool. I am burning up, Gertie moans, even though the night nursery is cool and dark. You can't remove her hair to check the apparatus of her brain, but you can try to feel her heart by poking your finger into the gap between her shoulders and her chest. I am on fire, she moans in that high little voice that's so hard to keep up. Somewhere on the street a dog begins to bark; in the back yard, Noodle I (family dachshund, 1951–60) barks back.

What is wrong with the girl? The butler holds her tongue down with a stick (Say ahhh!); he peers through a black cone at her eyes (Stop blinking!); he slides his handless wrist up under her dress (Breathe in . . . good . . . now out). He's checking to see if she has a soul, and when he doesn't find one, he makes her go to bed. Occasionally the mother wanders in, sticks a thermometer in her mouth, replaces an empty teacup with a full glass of ginger ale, removes the thermometer, leaves. At one point Henny appears to hang things in the closet.

The hangers rattle; the hated fluorescent light (built into the shelf over the bed) buzzes. What a waste, to have all the time in the world and all these things to read (*Katy Keene, Wuthering Heights, Little Lulu, Calling All Girls, Archie & Veronica, Little Women, Girl of the Limberlost, Seventeen*) and then be stuck with a pounding headache. Like the nerd in *The Twilight Zone* who survives atomic war and makes his way to a library only to break his glasses.

An impossible headache, and if aspirin won't touch it, then what? This is the fifties, a point midway between the future's great proliferation of remedies (Panadol, Excedrin, Tylenol, Aleve) and the past's (belladonna, leeches, horseradish, toads). In the fifties, there's only aspirin and a nervous mother. The father is always off voyaging to and from Atlantic City along the Blackhorse Pike, routinely pausing to buy Ginnie doll outfits (such as the maroon-and-gold drum majorette outfit his sick daughter's been hounding him for, complete with gold boots and baton) from pretty sales clerks. In the meantime the mother makes pudding. But any fool knows that if you want to live forever you shouldn't eat.

How hard to distinguish between my own voice speaking the part of mother or father or sister and the noises downstairs, ice cubes tinkling in highballs, the Westminster chimes waxing and waning, the television's giddy laughter as yet one more hapless couple tries to beat the clock.

Nor can I understand why my parents bother winding theirs, since they effectively consigned me to eternity just by giving me birth. Ding a ding dong, ding a ding dong. Forever and ever amen. It seemed, even then, a fate worse than death.

It's your fault, Edwin.

Don't Edwin me. You're the one with the weird blood type.

I should have listened to Mother. (Muth-ah: the accent something like the good witch's in *The Wizard of Oz*). The child's burning up and you're ...

Can I freshen your drink? Can I interest you in a sardine?

Can I interest you in a punch in the nose, Sis-tah? my sister says. How long has she been hiding there on the other side of the bedroom door, listening to me talking to myself?

Go away, I warn, don't you have something to do? But she insists she can't do anything as long as I keep on *talking*. It's getting on my nerves, she says, I'm telling Mom. You're always talking. It makes my nose bleed. When I ignore her she ups the ante. I'm telling, she warns, studying her bloody Kleenex with interest. I'm telling Benny Gold.

But if there's no empty space in the human body, then where on earth can Psyche hide? The ancients usually placed her in the liver or heart; during the Age of Enlightenment she moved to the pineal gland, in which Descartes claimed she "jigged like a balloon captive above a fire"; while practitioners of voodoo consign her to more retrievable quarters: umbilical cord, fingernail, lock of hair, etc. etc. And what about the story in the *National Enquirer* describing how someone weighed a body right before death, then right after, and figured that the difference (some endearingly precise amount—27/623's of an ounce?) was the weight of the soul? The soul herself had fled, though when she left remains unclear, since death would seem to be an ongoing process.

In any case it's humiliating to be caught talking to yourself.

Having PLAYED THE WESTMINSTER chimes straight through, the clock begins to strike. One, two, three, four … It's impossible to hear yourself think over all the racket, the sound of someone's (old Miss O'Rourke's?) mutt barking, the doorbell ringing, that infernal band. Still, what a relief to be standing upright at last, the sun so warm and flashing off the buttons on the men's uniforms, hundreds of bursts of light like a flock of chirping birds. No matter that your feet are sound asleep. Edwin! somebody shouts, waving toward the window.

Edwina! Mrs. Moss! Perhaps it isn't too late, though the horses are stamping their hooves and the train is due to depart at noon.

They look small, the horses; the people, especially the ones on horseback, smaller still. This is what makes action possible in the world of men. Like that moment when a plane starts to ascend and everything's on the verge of vanishing, and the cars and houses and swimming pools are getting reduced to blurry greenish brown rectangles. Then Ike snaps his fingers and the soldiers assemble, eager to make heroes of themselves, though anyone who's spent even an hour in the army could tell them it's an exercise in futility, sitting alone with a paring knife and a mountain of potatoes, reading between the lines of your beloved's latest missive, trying to locate in its lengthy description of a meal at Henri's (Prime Rib au Jus for Daddy, Dover Sole for Mommy, and guess what for me?), in its editorial zeal (target not targit and shooting has 1 T), some hint of affection.

But that was ages ago, in another lifetime. Henny, a young thing (imagine it!), almost as young as the Henny who's standing there on tiptoe at the edge of the crowd, straining to catch a glimpse of the men before they take off, as if it doesn't matter that someone's been frantically ringing the doorbell for hours, and the least she could do (since who're they going off to die for, anyway?) is answer it. Not to mention that the dog's digging up the garden and there's a putrid smell in the house. Go ahead and wave, shout till you're hoarse, it won't make any difference. Try reading between the lines of your smooth white palm: IF YOU WANT SOMETHING DONE, DO IT YOURSELF.

So must the housewife remain forever vigilant, in a constant state of readiness, sergeant-at-arms and surgeon ...

So must she know that if her potatoes are decaying it's because she failed to examine them weeks earlier when their tendency was to sprout, that noisome odors in her drains might be removed by applying three spoonfuls of chloride of lime dissolved in a cup of water, that the sensation of "pins and needles" might be avoided by eating whey in the morning, raisins at night. For every problem, a solution, or better yet, a preventative measure: why ask less of the author of *Lares and Penates, Home Truths?*

Why expect the house to cut her any slack, or give a damn that she was happier lying on the floor, her body stuffed to bursting with carbon-bearing fats, completely out of it? Fear always accompanies hope, just as there would appear to be no entirely suitable antidote to this condition, the surging of life back into sleeping limbs, the whole body jerking fitfully like a marionette operated by a lunatic. It's as if she's watching the small dark blur that is herself approach from far far away, whirring and spinning over the curved plain like a star or whirlwind, but growing clearer the closer it comes, a visual reversal of takeoff with the attendant feelings of trepidation and excitement, a blurred shape rapidly acquiring detail, miniature eyes, mouth, nose, all of which suddenly swell to what seems like mammoth proportion, and isn't it the sheer *size* of the runway that makes your heart pound, and not the physical jolt of wheels hitting earth?

Slowly she pulls herself away from the window; slowly she walks across the floor. A large woman, Edwina Moss, big-boned, with thick black hair and creamy white skin, a woman of the type usually called handsome. Nor is she accustomed to moving so sluggishly, to feeling herself so thoroughly drained of purpose, especially given the gravity of the occasion. At noon today her husband will be joining Mr. Lincoln's army, and the least she can do is put in an appearance. Wave a flag. Provide him with a basket supper for the journey. Why give fuel to the neighbors' smug conviction that Moss Cottage, despite its mistress' exalted reputation, is a monument to domestic misman-agement?

The third-floor hall is dim, its only source of light two small triangular windows, one cut in the north gable above the staircase, the other in the south. Whereas the east wall is without windows and slants sharply toward the roof peak, a feature of design intended to prevent ice from building around need-less cornicework, but with the unfortunate effect of making navigation difficult, even at the best of times. Something some-

thing something, where do you wander? Upstairs downstairs . . .
Edwina is an unusually tall woman; her eyesight is failing. Twice
she bumps her head on the eaves, trips over irregularities in the
floorboards.

Of course this is what happens when you try blaming
your bad mood on a house: it will turn right around and show
you who's boss. You can't make friends with it. That must be
why housewives need to invent endless projects, to trick themselves into thinking they aren't lonely.

Tentatively she feels her way down past the ticking clock
and the overflowing clothes hamper, then along the sun-
drenched second-floor hall, clumsily skirting the rosewood parrot stand (good morning good morning good morning) and
the empty dog bed, pausing to catch her breath by the hope
chest her husband carved for Gertie with his own hands, before
she negotiates the dark staircase leading to the kitchen. At some
point, probably while she herself was lying there like a beached
whale, Henny was up and busy: there's a little cake of glue melting in the tin glue pot, and the picnic basket's been removed
from its hook in the larder and is now neatly packed, a napkin
tucked around a warm loaf of bread, a slab of pâté, a wheel of
cheese, several ripe figs, an entire roast chicken. To look at the
basket now you'd never know that it once belonged to a gypsy
man with eyes like lumps of coal, who sharpened knives in exchange for his supper. He lived in a brightly painted wagon, in
the middle of the woods where it was forbidden to go, drawing
Edwina onward with his little silver flute.

Yet when did the hall become so long and dim and
crowded, endlessly long and impossibly dim and insanely
crowded with tidies and mats and fripperies, framed views of
this ruin or that, in flagrant contradiction of her own best ad-

vice about decoration and design? Whereas the basket suddenly seems oddly light, despite having been crammed full of food only moments earlier. Edwina holds it to her bosom as she walks, slowly at first and then picking up speed, moving more and more rapidly until she's almost running. It is human nature not to heed one's own advice, a little voice hisses, the airy hissing of gas from a lamp before the flame ignites. Shhh! Edwina hisses back.

Insolently, the basket rustles. Almost imperceptibly the hall curves to the left, a curve Edwina doesn't remember having noticed before, or certainly not here in Moss Cottage. There's a familiar smell, damp and earthy; briefly the walls glisten and exude sweat. For a moment everything's deathly still, as if time itself is hesitant to move forward ... and then the noise at the door starts up again, a pounding this time, louder than ever, and the next thing she knows she's in the vestibule, the fanlight is projecting a peacock's tail of sun onto the wall above the lowboy, and there's Pook, stiff-legged, hackles raised, letting out a series of deep, excited barks.

Back, Edwina orders, tugging on the door, the wood swollen from last night's rain. Look, it's Dr. Wingfield, she adds, gently caressing the indentations behind her dog's beautiful pointed ears, the place where the fur's as soft as a pup's and the skin slides thinly over the great basin of his skull. Mr. Goblin Head. Mr. Haymow. He's her ally, after all, the only member of the household who'll stick with her through thick and thin, though unfortunately not this morning. No, this morning (while *someone* was in the throes of a mysterious transformation) he was evidently bounding through the woods, his big heart beating like a kettledrum, his fur drenched and muddy, the sweet plume of his tail turning to a club of burdock. Smearing his muzzle with blood as well, meaning he either cut himself or killed something, probably the latter.

I came as soon as I was able, Dr. Wingfield says. How long has it been? Without removing his dark eyes from Edwina's face, he stoops to run one hand (in the wrong direction) along Pook's back, while gripping his leather bag tensely in the other. You should have gotten word to me sooner.

You took your own sweet time, Edwina replies. She grabs his wet hat and ·sets it on the lowboy between the pyramidal arrangement of pineapples and the silver card tray, then drapes his sodden greatcoat across the antlers of the stag her husband shot to punish Nature for trifling with his affections. It's crucial to take sides, Edwina reminds herself, thinking how there's nothing on earth that consoles her like the smell of Pook's wet coat, Pook's foul breath, even after he's been eating carrion. Unlike that other smell, the faintest trace of which keeps creeping into her nostrils from somewhere in the vicinity of the kitchen. *That* smell is repulsive. Follow me, she says, leading Dr. Wingfield, a lean man dressed as usual in a suit of black barathea, toward the front staircase.

Of course he's watching her body, its every move, with his insouciant shoe-button eyes. Just lift off the cap of long grayish hair and look into his head and you'll see they're on stalks like a doll's. But wasn't this always the problem with Simon Wingfield? He never left you alone, a desirable trait only during the early stages of courtship. Were you heating glue? he wonders as they round the second-floor landing. I ask because ...

Edwina doesn't hesitate. Clearly a lie's called for, since there will barely be time to deposit the doctor at Gertie's door before heading back downstairs. The household will be clamoring for food; Pook, too, will need to be fed. No, she tells him.

Indeed if the train's to depart at noon, she ought to be in the courtyard now, handing her husband the basket and kissing him one last time, albeit awkwardly, as he leans to embrace her from his saddle. There will be the tips of his mustache hairs, damp, prickly, unpleasantly suggestive. There will be that mole ... Oh, she ought to be with her husband, yet with every passing minute she's moving farther and farther away from him, back past the hope chest and the bird, the clock and the little triangular window, along the dark hallway to Gertie's door.

Inside the room everything is precisely as she left it, the bag of rue at the threshold emitting its prophylactic aroma of coconut milk, the mahogany four-poster veiled like a bride against the midday sun, the panade in its Quimper bowl resting untouched on the nightstand. No, nothing has changed, but isn't that to be expected in a house turned hospital, time either expanding hugely, each second an endless gray ocean, gray clouds above, heaving gray swells below, or too tiny to measure, a minnow swallowed by a whale? Surely even Simon Wingfield won't be able to find cause for complaint. Or at least nothing aside from that snarl of dust and hair under the clothes tree, Henny evidently refusing to mop up anything so closely resembling herself.

Gertie too hasn't moved an inch but is still lying there thin as a wafer in her gauze tent, gazing blankly at the ceiling, her brilliant red curls corkscrewing this way and that across the pillow slip. The arrangement of the curls is apparently random yet strikes Edwina as artful, not unlike the angle of her jaw, its irritating upward thrust. Every now and then her breathing quickens, her eyes flick from side to side, and her hands bunch into fists. Briefly her mouth cracks open, a pink sliver of tongue emerges to moisten her lips, and Edwina marvels at the silent operation of Gertie's will, frozen in place like an enormous fish at the bottom of her soul.

Hmmmm, Dr. Wingfield says, drawing the curtain. Of course the daughter serves as an advertisement for everything the mother once was, though there can't be any comparison between Gertie's slim luminosity and Edwina's opaque bulk, a kid torso stuffed with grit and nailparings. Hmmmm, Dr. Wingfield says again, glancing at the untouched panade, its thinly shivering crust. His face is covered with a faint sheen, but who knows whether from the exertion of the climb or moisture in the air. He inserts a thermometer in Gertie's mouth. When did she last eat? he asks, and Edwina realizes she can't remember. It's been so chaotic, she reminds him. The knocking, the barking, the people in the courtyard. No to mention Henny's thumb. For suddenly she recalls noticing an enormous gauze bandage like the knob on a baton, alarmingly apparent when Henny waved her little flag.

And then she smiles, suddenly cheered. The basket. How could she have forgotten the basket? Clutched to her breast, perfect evidence of maternal devotion. But I've brought dinner, she says. You see? A basket full of her favorite things. And there's the Flemish doll lying on the floor, none the worse for wear despite a missing head; and there's Pook lying nearby, panting, in that position dogs assume to mimic a side view of a standing dog.

Miss Moss, Simon Wingfield says. Wake up! He claps his hands in Gertie's face, but she doesn't flinch. You may not be aware of it, he tells Edwina, but I've read your books, every one of them. I know, as you so eloquently put it, that an invalid should never be teased with the exertion of making a decision.

Except she's already made one, Edwina replies. Besides, in

my experience, men prefer stories of adventure. Men and women, she sighs, a hopeless combination, and for a moment she finds herself remembering a summer night years ago, the distracted look on young Simon Wingfield's face just after he finished kissing her. Standing at the edge of the dance pavilion, the band playing a plaintive air she couldn't quite make out, the summer meteor showers raining down on the glistening black surface of Egg Pond. Simon's eyes also, glistening and black ... Shhh! he was saying. *Necturus maculosus,* over there in the reeds. The female. You rarely get to see them, they're so clever at camouflage.

And all at once it's as if she's watching her own soul swim toward her through the shallow ooze, setting in dreamlike motion the filmy ruff of gills that sprout from either side of its pale moonlike head. It's almost come, her soul is saying, the hapless time, when the speech of Nature arises only in faint, spent echoes; when the fire of the salamander shall once more kindle ...

The doctor, meanwhile, has been holding forth on the subject of sponge baths, hinting that Edwina's done more harm than good by catering to Gertie's whim. The girl's heart and lungs are healthy, in fact he sees nothing to indicate illness. Whim, he repeats, plucking the thermometer from Gertie's chapped lips with his elegant fingers, consulting it wearily before shaking it down. I understand it's become a fad among girls of a certain age. The Welsh Fasting Girl—is Edwina familiar with the case? Sarah Jacob of Pencander began by eating acorn-sized pieces of apple, then smaller and smaller portions until she was chewing and swallowing air. When you get hungry enough, he says, staring pointedly at Gertie, you will eat. No one can go without food forever, not even a stubborn little girl.

The influence of the Spiritualists, he adds sourly. I'm surprised you'd permit them in your house.

Edwina is puzzled. But I haven't, she says. I don't even know who they are. She watches as the doctor moves away from the bed and stands by the window. I don't suppose it would hurt to give her a tonic, he says, casting a rueful gaze across the pond, as if he too were feeling the long-dead breeze of a long-past night, the quickening beat of Edwina's girlish heart. Midnight, the wind's hand passing over the water (be still be still), the moon pasted to the sky, a dark flat thing with nothing behind it except the angled ceiling you bump your head on if you're not careful. Oh, it's a scientific fact: put them in proximity and hearts will beat in unison, which is why if you get too close to someone you can lose track of which heart is which. You can begin thinking you *are* the other person, mother or father, sister or lover. And if that heart is broken ...

Edwina can hear the sound of the gypsy's flute, and once again she feels an enormous drowsiness overtaking her, only this time she tries to resist it. Whenever she abandons consciousness it's harder and harder to retrieve, and after she does, something is invariably missing.

... AND MIGHTN'T I AT LAST LEAVE BEHIND FOR-
ever all discussion of man's progress from huntsman to herder
to farmer, from savage to gastronome, from the Paleo-Indian
ripping meat off a mastodon's thigh to the vigilant gaveuse
coaxing through a slot in its belly the goose's silk purse of liver;
at last forgo all talk about the art of cookery, the clarification of
stocks and the ripening of cheeses, the vitamin content of beet
greens and the storage life of rutabagas, the utility of brass
weights, the virtues of wood-fired stoves, the pleasurable dis-
covery of fiddleheads after a spring rain, mushrooms after an
autumn storm—mightn't I now at last confess, once and for all,
that it is too late, TOO LATE, the night dark and windswept,
the shutters banging against the dark windows of a room where
a child awakens terrified in a pool of sweat, a girlchild upon
whom a mortal illness like a wayward caravan has descended
while she lies sleeping, the horses' necks flecked with foam, the
gypsy coachman's eyes burning, a knife clenched between his
teeth, as all the while round and round the night nursery, past
the clothes tree and the bookshelves and the Flemish doll, the
brightly painted carts careen, the wheels squealing on their
axles, the curb chains rattling, and can I admit after a lifetime of
pointless reflection on bain-maries and daubieres that I've been
brought at long last to the threshold of my terror, to confront

at last the fleeting gift of appetite, the rapt adoration of the gaveuse for her doomed flock of geese, the loving way she inserts white corn one kernel at a time through those avid yellow beaks, strokes those soft feathered breasts, urges her geese toward their mysterious destiny, the day on which the transformation is complete, when an organ designed to remove food's impurities is transformed into food itself, when the foie gras can be poached in a solution called with no apparent trace of irony "the mother," as if there's no ultimate difference between womb and cauldron, as if to be a mother is to court doom, to cook the little bowls full of porridge, to nourish the limbs and stroke the hair and kiss the overbright cheeks ...

WHAT DOES THE MOTHER *DO* ALL DAY long in the kitchen? What on earth does she do?

Though maybe she isn't doing anything; maybe that just happens to be where she ended up along with the pup-in-a-basket, the lawn mower, the beautiful hand-painted wooden table the Kecks brought back from Germany, the blue-and-white-checked placemats, one of the three mattresses, the plastic lid filled with barley, the celluloid butler, the immense china goose. Oh, also the sink, which she's propped against, facing away from it, away from the three pewter salt spoons resting on the drainboard, and toward the window. Her temples are throbbing. You can try adding things to your life to make it sweeter, smoke a cigarette, for instance, watch a show on television, drink a little gin, but after a while nothing works. A boyfriend? Do you see any boyfriends here? Sure, you can have children, but they'll go away to school, and the school will be unimaginably strange and remote, a shoe box maybe, in the basement, the backyard, another universe, the teacher a giant. Your children will stop treating you tenderly. Worse, their heads will fall off.

You can't tell by looking at her face, but the mother is completely flipped out. During the hurricane a child plunged from the edge of the world, which is to say from the maple dresser and into a beaded moccasin where it got smooshed by a giant foot, which is to say a child died. Not her own, but still . . . And now to her everlasting shame she finds herself wondering what if it *had been* hers, as if she can somehow get the jump on tragedy by imagining a world without a single thing in it she couldn't bear to lose. The next thing she knows her older daughter's come down with tuberculosis. Of course this is the same impulse that drives the mother to drain the gin bottle once it's been opened, as well as what led her to sneak into the kitchen of the house on Lindholm Lane and, having located the white box on top of the refrigerator, to eat every last petit four, starting with one of each type, and then devouring them row by row, pink, yellow, green, blue, until the box was absolutely empty, not a single thing left, not even that Tinkerbell-like creature who figures in one of her favorite myths.

After you open something, you're responsible for what comes out: sorrow and sickness, fear and pestilence. A cake. A child. But just try tricking the gods by eating all the cakes, and your skin and eyeballs will turn bright yellow. Or at least that's what happened to the mother when she was a girl on Lindholm Lane, ditto a grown-up woman on Boxwood Road. The gods go for the liver. Look at Prometheus. It wasn't enough to give men fire, he had to teach Zeus a lesson. Butcher an ox, he ordered, and make two piles, hiding the best cuts under a foul heap of guts, the bones and gristle under a blanket of snow-white fat. Zeus will always choose form over content, Prometheus promised, and the next thing he knew he was chained to a rock, an eagle was eating his liver, and Pandora was getting ready to open her famous box.

The message is clear: try blurring the distinction between altar and dinner table and you end up chained to a rock that is both. No wonder all the mother's stories have food-related crimes at their heart. They scare the older daughter though she has no clue why. She hasn't figured it out yet: if the idea is to end up with nothing, where does that leave her?

Just because the house is a little house inside a big house doesn't mean it escapes the gods' notice.

The mother has a variety of options: she can smoke or drink or watch television (a domino sawed in half, good luck). When she looks out the window all she sees is yellow, an expanse of yellow quilt. That and the hind end of a yellow autograph hound, DADDY printed in big letters under the tail. It's very sad for the mother to be who she is, propped against the sink. We'll have Mrs. Paul's fish sticks for dinner, she decides. Also hearts of lettuce. Tartar sauce *and* Russian dressing, since the older daughter who detests them both because they remind her of vomit isn't around to complain now is she? Gone gone gone, everyone gone, even the younger daughter whose friend Patience's mother has taken them to Mermaid Lake, where by now they've all probably caught polio, thank you very much. Okay, not fish sticks but a martini and *And Then There Were None*. A manicure and pedicure. She will spoil herself, if no one else will.

Meanwhile where exactly *is* this DADDY? Headed down the White Horse Pike, the Black Horse Pike in his brand-new Dodge? Such romantic names, the roads that radiate from town. On yet another "business trip" to Atlantic City, prowling the boardwalk as the Ferris wheel begins revolving on its gold spokes, and Nora Devine begins applying lipstick in a windowpane almost dark enough to be a mirror, monitoring the approach through her pursed lips of a sexy man whose white shirt is open at the neck, sleeves rolled to just below the elbow, whistling . . .

Of course he doesn't really exist, the father. There was a father who was part of the original set, until the dachshund ate him; that's why the father's never home. Occasionally a finger (pointer) takes his part, the rude middle finger, though taller, being reserved for the grandmother's rare visits. And yet how well I remember his actual hands, curly black hair growing on either side of the knuckles and skin the color of cream with an even paler band where the wedding ring had been before the nursing home aide gave it to me for safekeeping, since it would appear that in our dotage many of us turn into thieves.

First he buys my mother a box of saltwater taffy, even though she doesn't like sweets and has been wearing dentures since her late twenties. Then he buys my sister a shot glass with a picture on it of a bullethole (I GOT SMASHED IN ATLANTIC CITY) and a pair of wax lips, confirming my grandmother's view that he lacks judgment. In the air the smell of buttered popcorn, spun sugar, hot pitch. Low tide and the ratcheting whine of a sewing machine stitching names on sailor caps, merry-go-round music, the plaintive cries of gulls.

My father's thirsty and he's happy. He's so happy to be away from my mother's sorrow, my sister's nosebleeds, my lungs. It's as if all the women of Atlantic City know he's headed their way, as if they're all beautiful, my father a plump amorous Vronsky, a good dancer to boot. Oh yes, before the carpet was wall-to-wall, before the thunderbolt sliced him in two, he used to guide my ungainly body across the living room, the music slow and oddly nostalgic, given it came from a time we hadn't left behind yet. "Stairway to Heaven"? And meanwhile there was my mother looking on, her face stiff, taking little sips of her manhattan, sliding pretzels off the ceramic dachshund's "tail," struck mute by the fact that as females we shared a pliancy so obviously sexual as to make us forever embarrassed in each other's presence.

In the Sands Hotel the pretty desk clerk hands my father his keys. Can I prevail upon you, he asks (one of his favorite locutions), to show me to my room? and the girl blushes, rings for the bellhop. The night is young, the ocean inching closer and closer to the boardwalk's pitch-smeared pilings, clutching wildly at them as if the farther it creeps from its own pitch-dark heart, the better chance it has of escaping the little salt mill left there by a drowned sailor, grinding out salt from now until the end of time. Will that be all, sir? the bellhop asks, depositing the suitcase on the luggage rack, pocketing his tip, closing the door behind him. Nora Devine is cooling her heels in the ballroom. She's nowhere near as smart as the mother but who needs brains to dance?

Nor does the mother seem to be exercising her intelligence back at home now, either. Indeed back at home everything's an awful mess. Two of the black border tiles and four of the yellow tiles have fallen off the kitchen wall but you don't see the mother gluing them on again, do you? The tiles have fallen off and left pale blue holes, the color the kitchen was in 1918. In those days the mother was more elegant, in no danger of going bald because her head and hair and neck and shoulders were all of a piece, smooth elegant porcelain, unlike the current mother, who has less hair than the brand-new (and frighteningly large) baby, and whose right leg is coming unraveled. Now there's mold on the meat-cakes; a parrot in the icebox. It's harder to do nothing than something, said Mrs. Beeton, but she was a paragon of industry.

Still, if the mother could be persuaded to put a little effort into sprucing the place up or making dinner ... Better yet, if she could actually pull herself together long enough to bake a cake from scratch! It's not as if she doesn't know how, or that there isn't an entire section of *The American Woman's Cook Book* dedicated to the subject: One-Two-Three-Four Cake. Lady Baltimore Cake. "We need no words for Devil's Food Cake. Always a favorite—easy to bake."

And if she runs into trouble? Then she'll get the butler to help her out. As usual he's right there beside her in the kitchen, and though he only has one hand and his nose is staved in, giving him a perpetually sorrowful and slightly crazed look, he also happens to be a great cook. The great Antonin Carême, in fact, who, according to the grandmother, has fed kings and queens, statesmen and courtesans, the Emperor Napoleon and his sullen bride—one of the greatest pastrycooks of all time, who will die before he reaches the age of fifty, consumed by the fire of his genius and the coals of his ovens.

"THE FINE ARTS ARE FIVE IN NUMBER," said Antonin Carême, "painting, sculpture, poetry, music, architecture. And the main branch of architecture is confectionary." Which is to say, if the house where you were born offends you, why not build a house of cake? Or at least that's the conclusion young Antonin came to not long after being abandoned by his father on the floor of a tavern near the Paris city gate.

It was 1790. The Revolution was over, but no one was happy. The tavern stank of bitterness, urine, sweat. From time to time the door flew open, letting in blasts of snow-scented air, sending the drinkers closer to the fire while at the same time luring the boy away from it and toward the door. Dark shop windows as far as the eye could see, stretching the length of the street, their sills piled high with snow. It was a brutally cold night; no one but a fool would venture outdoors. Yet when at last a cloaked man entered with the blazing face of a morphine addict, and with him the subtle scent of browning onions, the boy made his escape.

What had his father said when he deposited him on that cold stone floor among the shit-caked clogs, raveling gray hose, and louse-specked breeches of the former lower classes? "Go, little one! This is the time of fine fortunes; it only needs wit to make one, and wit you have. Perhaps this evening or tomorrow some fine house will open its doors to you. Leave us behind; misery is our lot and we must die of misery."

The boy sniffed. Though he was in no other respect like a dog (being unusually fastidious, and more interested in building food than smelling it), he had a keen nose. Oh, there may have been a blizzard blowing that fateful night, but within the wind's icy folds Antonin Carême picked up the thin scent of onion that lured him from the tavern and followed it to its source: a rude gargote three doors down where in exchange for a few sous you could get a ladle of undistinguished marmite, a bit of bread. I will work for my supper, the boy suggested; Mme. Aubain handed him a knife and a chicken. It needs gutting, she told him, and the rest is history.

Young Antonin learned quickly. He learned, for example, how to render a nub of lard and let the onion sweat, exuding its latent sugar, then to fan the fire until the caramelizing juices began to release their enticing smell, at which point he'd open the window. But no sooner had he perfected Mme. Aubain's trick for snaring customers than he'd been snatched away by another establishment, slightly more respectable, one of the earliest restaurants in fact, its birth yet another result of the Revolution. The newly unemployed cooks of the newly deposed rich had to make a living too after all.

Mme. Aubain was brokenhearted: there was no M. Aubain, and Antonin, in addition to being a much better cook than she was, happened to be very nice-looking. Indeed by the time he left the gargote Antonin Carême had shot up into a tall and lithe young man with a refined, skeptical expression; a handsome youth whose lofty ambitions were happily matched by true creative genius. Nor should his quick ascent from the

rank slum where he was born come as a surprise. Hadn't his father said that of all his children, this one's prospects seemed
rosiest? He said that and then he was gone, leaving his son to
watch his shabby coattails retreat down a snow-shrouded alley-
way. The truth is, Carême was too smart to keep; he made his
parents nervous, and he knew it.

Of course historic accounts focus on cuisine rather than
psyche, but it certainly seems likely that young Antonin would
have wanted revenge, and revenge on three fronts. Thus the
blazing comet of his career can be seen as a means of exacting
revenge on his parents; the inherently pernicious nature of his
medium, on his patrons; the perfection of his work, on God.
Which is not to say that he lacked charm, or that he didn't love
to cook, only that there could be no stopping him. This is what
happens when, however sweet and complex and miraculously
deft the houses you erect out of sugar and flour and butter,
there is no escaping the house where you were born. The problem is, a house of cake is still a house.

All of which might serve to explain the events of 1 April
1802, during the state dinner honoring First Consul (soon to be
Emperor) Napoleon Bonaparte. The Treaty of Amiens had just
been signed, the Consul was in a party mood, and Carême, hard
on the heels of his eighteenth birthday, had been entrusted with
the creation of a series of pièces montées, elaborate sotelties for
the Consul's amusement.

In those days a formal dinner was nothing like what Edwina Moss would have served, let alone what we're used to now.
You weren't supposed to devote your attention to single elements trotted out sequentially, a limpid consommé garnished
with lemon grass for instance, followed by trout on a bed of
wilted field greens, etc. etc. In those days people didn't diet, and

the gourmand (i.e. candidate for apoplexy) was a physiologic ideal.

So you might imagine the table, every inch of it crammed, its perimeter with guests, its surface with decorative objects (gleaming gold and silver candelabra, pyramids of pineapples and peaches and plums and muscat grapes, elaborate floral displays, cruets and salt dishes and whole small trees clipped to resemble nymphs and satyrs and foodstuffs), not to mention the foods themselves (soup-filled tureens in the shape of lobsters and rabbits and waterfowl, silver platters raised to varying heights on ornamental silver pediments and containing poularde à la périgourdine, boeuf en daube, entire fish such as golden eyebrow poached in aspic, poached skate liver, vol au vent of spinal marrow, galantine of eel arranged in coils like a rattler with its pomegranate-seed eye coyly peeking up at the hungry dinner guest, towering cakes made to resemble Turkish pavilions, Venetian waterfalls, Irish ruins, with tasty Demoiselles D'Honneur at their feet ...).

Nothing got passed around; where you sat determined what you ate, and you were, yourself, wedged into your chair, barely able to move. Perhaps you were fortunate and your portion of the dimly candlelit table actually contained some delectable morsel. Or maybe you ended up stuck between two huffing and mountainous gobble-guts, behind a mountain of waxed fruit.

Though never fear, for what I've just described was merely the first course, the prelude.

It's a mild evening in the spring of 1802. Through the open windows of Malmaison can be heard the wind stirring the lilacs, the plashing of fountains, the song of the nightingale.

Servants creep in, softly, softly. The Revolution is over, but still you don't want a great banging of china and cutlery, undue attention called to your own refuse, to the partly chewed bones and moist pits and gobbets of fat left on your plate. As the servants silently clear the table, roll up the now-filthy cloth revealing a fresh one beneath, the Consul claps his hands to signal the start of the entremets. Naturally he's seated at the head of the table, but would Josephine be sitting at his right hand or would someone like, say, Lord Nelson occupy that place? Unlikely, given the uneasiness of the truce between the two nations, though the British ambassador's no doubt in attendance, as well as dignitaries from Spain and the Netherlands.

Josephine, then, at Napoleon's side. And to her right? Charles-Maurice de Talleyrand, the club-footed Prince de Bénévent and Carême's future employer? Or better yet, gimlet-eyed Pierre Laclos, who can be counted on to amuse with gossip from both the front and the salon? Possibly Marc-Antoine Désaugiers, the gastronomic poet ("I wish to be buried under the tablecloth/ Between four large dishes")? In any event a full complement of witty, beautiful women (including David's languid subject, the doe-eyed Juliette Récamier; Talleyrand's former mistress and now wife, the heiress Catherine Grande; the Consul's spoiled baby sister, Marie-Pauline, affianced to Camillo Borghese; the celebrated painter Élisabeth Vigée-Lebrun, a frequent guest though no great admirer of the Consul's politics), as well as an equal number of charming and powerful men.

But make haste! Our Amphitryon is growing impatient, as is Josephine's young orangutan, who, in formal dress at the foot of the table, is once again copying the Consul's every move. Clap clap! goes Napoleon. Clap clap! goes the orangutan. Food isn't really the point, a fact of which Carême is well aware. For like most narcissists, the Consul prefers those monuments to his glory which will prove more durable than, for instance, a boned eel. This is why the Consul is an ardent admirer of architecture over cuisine, and why he and Carême make a perfect match.

As for the architect of this feast, why there he is hiding in the wings, taking one last withering look at the plans he worked on into the wee hours of the morning. Carême's drawings are obsessively, even sickeningly detailed, since he can't seem to shake the idea of a link between thoroughness and viability, as if this is how gods operate, making worlds. He sighs, runs a hand through his short black curls. The people at the table—idiots, all of them, laughing at that insufferable monkey—don't have a clue. Of course that's the difference between food and art: the former can literally kill you, which explains its unspeakable power.

There is a flourish of trumpets and the musicians enter, their robes amaranth, the deep cockscomb red that is Napoleon's favorite, the color of immortality. The entremets is about to begin. At last the exhausted diners may unbutton a button here, a button there, secretively expel what gas they can, nibble stalks of fennel and pick their teeth in preparation for the yet more lavish second course. The flutes embroider on an oriental motif; an enormous wheeled trolley rolls in, invisible beneath poppy-orange drapes, and on it a Greek temple made of fondant-iced pain de Gênes, its almond flavor commemorating the Genoans' wretched diet before they surrendered to Napoleon. The music intensifies and the portico swings open. The statue of a beautiful woman stands half-dressed in a cockleshell, spilling spun sugar water from a marzipan box. But is it some trick of light or is the water actually moving? And how is it possible that the statue is able to step from the fountain and approach the Consul's table?

Look, he says, a stunning likeness! For though the statue's expression is impassive and its gait more graceful than that of the original, its white chiton is uncannily like Josephine's, its coiffure identical. A living woman, Talleyrand pronounces, made to look like paste. An allegory of diplomacy, replies Laclos, a real woman trying to pass herself off as a creature of artifice on an artificial fountain trying to pass itself off as real. But when he reaches out to "taste" the gown and accidentally brushes against the statue's hand, he's horrified to see a finger fall to the floor and shatter.

Is she tormenting him? asks Pauline, when the statue sets the box at the Consul's feet and smiles invitingly. She has never liked her sister-in-law. No, don't you see? replies Catherine Grand. It's the story of Pandora. She isn't supposed to open the box, but of course she will. A woman who refuses to open a present is no woman at all but ... A gift from the gods! finishes Laclos.

Meanwhile the box has been positioned over an opening in the trolley, and the trolley over a hole in the floor, making it possible for dish after dish to fly up out of it (suspended on wires? in any event somehow borne aloft to the table): the so-called pièces de résistance of the second course. These dishes usually share a common element; in this case they're made from a single three-hundred-pound West Indian turtle, in honor of Josephine's Creole heritage. How astonishing the way dishes keep swarming up out of that box! Deviled neck meat of turtle, turtle quenelles light as air, sautéed turtle kidneys and grilled turtle steaks, nageoires (flippers) de tourtue (à l'américaine, à la financière, à l'indienne), boiled stomach of turtle, roasted back of turtle, poached turtle eggs, an entire turtle shell filled with a rich potage de tortue, the head and lights boiled with two whole bottles of Madeira, quantities of sweet Isigny butter, as well as parsley, bay, thyme, basil, marjoram, minced ham, anchovies, cayenne pepper, pimiento, cloves, mace. Hardly the "absence d'épices" Lady Morgan complained of in 1829, nor would James Joyce ("God made food, the Devil invented seasoning") have considered Carême a saint.

Oh too too ghastly! says Mlle. Vigée-Lebrun, though she's laughing. If these are supposed to be the cursed fruits of Pandora's curiosity, then surely we can't be expected to *eat* them!

Of course it's intended to amuse, but the joke is lost on the Consul. For wasn't Pandora sent by the gods to punish human appetite? And isn't amaranth the color of blood? And what exactly is it scripture claims "shall be raised incorruptible"? Clearly every bite you take hastens the breakdown of flesh, and if it was the Devil who invented seasoning, wasn't he trying as usual to cover something up? Anxious, the Consul surveys the faces of his guests (and what are they staring at like that, their expressions amazed?) lining the perimeter of his table, its uncannily symmetrical spread of dishes, everything paired. Hah! thinks the Consul, for with just such attention to design does Nature spread her rust and rot and ruin. It's as if even at this moment of triumph he can see down the long corridor of the years to Elba, the empire overthrown, his wasted life . . .

And then all at once he realizes the object of his guests' attention. It's Josephine, Josephine who has been truly undone by the entremets, Josephine who is sitting there with tears pouring silently down her cheeks.

The flippers, she whispers, shaken by sobs. Ma pauvre . . .

But she is lost, thinking back to a day in her long ago and happy childhood, a trip home from St. Lucia in her brother's fishing boat and there beside them the shadow of a huge turtle drawing itself through the blue-green water with its beautiful green flippers. Such delicate appendages to propel so big a creature! How could anyone bring themselves to cut off such delicate—such *brave!*—appendages? To cut them off and then to cook them and cover them with sauce? Let alone to eat them?

Heartbroken, she is truly heartbroken—this is what food will do to you.

(The mother, for instance, is leaving the house with her little girls to take them for their annual checkup, and it isn't so much that she's been sneaking vanilla extract from its hiding place inside the grandfather clock, causing her to forget that the last time they got shots their arms had to be sewed back on, or that she's left a pot of split pea soup boiling on the stove, for when you think about it, really, isn't that the butler's job?—but that when upon their return she exclaims OH NUTS I'VE BURNT THE PEAS, and her older daughter begins to sob uncontrollably, she finds the reaction both alarming and repellent though not surprising, since after all this is the child who names her pets for foods, Potato and Carrot, Cupcake and Cocoa, Noodle ...)

And afterward the turtle would have used her flippers to haul her unwieldy self onto the moonlit beach, to make a furrow where she could deposit her eggs. The beach silver in the moonlight, the waves gently thumping the shore. No doubt she'd have been so preoccupied she wouldn't have heard the men sneaking up from behind, dropping the net over her, until it was too late. In the silver moonlight they'd have prepared her for shipment, turned her on her back and bound her flippers, an essential measure if she weren't to exhaust herself by thrashing about or to damage her tender undershield. No attempt would be made to force her en route if she refused to eat, but this wouldn't constitute a hardship, since Green Turtles can easily go for six weeks without food, and for three weeks or more without losing weight.

Tell me what you eat; I will tell you what you are, said Brillat-Savarin (anticipating the sixties slogan), but he never meant that we should identify with our food, as was clearly the case with Josephine and the turtle, as well as with the older daughter and the peas.

From Martinique to LeHavre, and then overland in a carriage, sewn into a burlap bag lined with excelsior and dried seaweed, only to be delivered at last into the hands of that man standing there in a tall white hat, who stabbed her in the neck and caught her blood in a bucket. Martinique to LeHavre to Paris! Such a long journey, and for what? First the man removed from the upper shell the gelatinous dull green meat which is called calipash, then from the lower the yellowish meat which is called calipee.

There he is now, watching, pleased to see that his vision (the pristine surface of the cake cracking apart to reveal a reptilian nightmare of dinner within) hasn't been lost on everyone. Though who would have guessed it would be the Consul's wife he'd move to tears? The Empress-to-be has never been Carême's type; she is too petulant, too infantile, too interested in stealing scenes. When the setting is a dinner party, the cook should be the most powerful (albeit least visible) person there. Besides, Carême likes his women as white and smooth and sweet as the blancmange for which he will one day become famous.

Antonin Carême! You have to admit there's something magnetic about that face, that wryly melancholic smile, those luminous dark eyes monitoring the approach of a nightmare you can actually sink your teeth into. A face that combines the best features of Heathcliff (i.e. the young Laurence Olivier) with the best features of the butler (i.e. everything the plump, amorous father is not). You'd never catch Antonin Carême dancing the night away in the arms of a pretty shopgirl, and then taking her back to his hotel room to fuck. Not Antonin Carême. If he has dark circles under his eyes it's from having spent night after sleepless night perfecting every single element of this soteltie, from the expansive palladian portico of frosted pain de Gênes (white as snow, smooth and white, SMOOTH AND WHITE!) down to the gilded egg the Empress-to-be has just found lodged in a corner of the box and has fished out with her nimble fingers.

Look! she says, smiling, holding up the little golden ball on the palm of her hand.

That would be Hope, Laclos explains, whereupon the Consul urges her to crack it open, saying there's bound to be a prize of some sort inside, a special treat, a bibelot or a particularly dainty morsel ...

The orangutan suddenly plucks a louse from the nape of the poet's neck, stares at it, and puts it in its mouth. Gorguh, it says.

Yes, prompts Catherine Grand, you must open it immediately. We cannot stand the suspense a second longer.

Of course that's the essence of Hope. And when you do crack the shell, all that emerges is a bad smell, a little yellowish powder, a shriveled black hatchling.

WHICH IS WHY IT ISN'T A GOOD IDEA
to put your eggs in one basket. Sooner or later someone or
something will catch your eye—in my case the doll sitting in
the antique store window—and before you know it you're ma-
rooned with your obsession, unable to sleep, and lonelier than
ever. I don't remember the store's name; it appeared for the
briefest of instants, a phantasmagoric bazaar, as if its sole purpose were to deliver the doll into my arms and then vanish, replaced by a depressing rug-cleaning establishment.

The doll was Flemish, meaning she came from Flanders,
where the poppies grew; to get a good look at her I had to
stand on one of the metal sidewalk grates my mother called
accidents waiting to happen. About two feet tall, she was
dressed in a tailored suit made of twill and faded to a pleasing
luna-moth shade of green, its seams strained by the sawdust-
stuffed block of her torso. In the gap between the wide piqué
lapels, just above the embroidered collar of the blouse, a quarter inch of grayish kidskin emerged and then a disturbing rift,
the place where the kid body and the bisque neck were joined.
Her hair was fuzzy, yellow, her least attractive feature (that is,
until you removed the white lace pantaloons). On her feet tiny
high-button shoes of brown glove leather, moth-eaten lisle
stockings. Two full-length slips, one cotton, the other muslin,

for warmth. She wasn't of this century. She was prohibitively expensive, and she reminded me of Joy, her face pellucid and faintly podgy, the mindless innocence of her blue glass eyes belied by the nutcrackerish gleam of her teeth. I thought I'd die if I couldn't have her.

Your father isn't made of money, my mother said when I came groveling, not to defend but to indict him. At this point (the period immediately following what we referred to as the accident) he no longer sold televisions or dishwashers, though my sister and I still used the decks of cards backed with his former employers' logos for our protracted games of war on the living room carpet. Indeed this may have been during one of several periods in my childhood when my father was out of work and, having no good excuse to leave home, feeling melancholy, trapped.

You have enough dolls, my mother said, pouring split peas into the pot with the ham bone and clove-studded onion. Then she looked at the clock over the door into the dining room. The sound of a ball repeatedly hitting the garage wall was interrupted by the arrival of my father's car, its door slamming. Hey there Mr. D! Hey there Joey! Come on, my mother said. I'll just set this on simmer. We can get cherry Cokes afterward, but don't tell Daddy. And not if you embarrass me like you did before. The poor nurse was only trying to do her job.

Of course by the time we got home the house was full of smoke, foul black smoke everywhere. Oh nuts, my mother said, I've burned the peas, and she opened the vent over the stove (murderer murderer), but not before I'd started sobbing. Insubstantial, ghostly, that's how my lungs had appeared in the X ray Dr. Keck whisked away before I could get a good look, gauzy like the organdy curtains that the summer breezes tugged through all our windows, open wide to let out smoke. Old Miss O'Rourke for instance, as Muffin hauled her along the sidewalk from bush to bush, was confirmed in her belief that ours was a house of ghosts.

I imagined the peas hurt and no one there to do a thing. Joy hurt and no one there either. As for the doll, eventually her head would crack when Henny pulled the maple dresser away from the wall to plug in the vacuum cleaner. I admit, the distinction blurred. In any event the whole system was bad, promoting either excessive caution or utter heedlessness.

I ended up in the children's ward of the hospital where Joy got her stitches. From my bed I could see sick bodies shuttle by, their features cloudy and dismal, for who needed features now that the world was about to end?

Meanwhile no one would admit what was wrong with me, and like any avid fan of the *Reader's Digest* (little girls all over America, perfectly healthy one minute, dying of cancer the next), I assumed the worst. Tests, my mother explained. Dr. Keck says you have to eat if you want to get better. Better than what, Mother dah-ling? (Except, really, I said nothing, to provide my testers with the least possible evidence.) I brought Jell-O, she persisted. Your favorite, red with fruit cocktail. Extra maraschino cherries. No bananas. (But I wasn't eating, either.) My father refused to look me in the eye, but stood peering through a window tinted so the sky seemed like a tropical lagoon. He was smoking; you could do that in hospitals then, no one would stop you, even if your daughter had TB. After all, it never stopped the residents of the Magic Mountain. My parents brought red Jell-O and a plant and a nurse outfit for my Ginny doll. They didn't bring my sister though; to be on the safe side they'd left her home, going on the assumption that one daughter was better than none.

My parents. No sooner had they arrived than they were leaving. I could picture them back in the car, my mother shakily reapplying the lipstick she'd smudged when she placed a quick kiss atop my head, my father lighting up again, both of them heaving huge sighs of relief. Brilliant red sun falling behind the willows and into the Wissahickon ... Sun under (above? at least in some key relationship to) a yardarm.

Later, when Dr. Keck appeared with his clipboard and stethoscope I was glad to see him, while he for his part seemed nicer than usual, having been at last justified in his suspicion that there was something fundamentally wrong with me. Medium height with a crewcut, pinkish skin, and a raw protuberant brow, a receding forehead, just like his son, whereas Polly took after her mother, a great beauty. Feel up to another visitor? Dr. Keck asked. It's after hours, but ...

And so it was that Benny Gold came stalking in with the Flemish doll in his arms, his glassy eyes not unlike hers, though more brightly inquisitive than mindlessly innocent. Dramatic too, he paused for a moment, clad in the usual chinos and navy-issue turtleneck, and as he did those glassy eyes swept the length and breadth of the room, taking in its yellow flowered wallpaper, its stuffed animals and balloons and posies, its two rows of four beds each, reddish sun shining on the white metal bars and silver crank handle of the bed opposite (belonging to a cute raven-haired boy who'd just had a hernia operation), ditto my own bed and my bedtray where beside a Pyrex loaf pan of red Jell-O, a peacock-shaped planter put forth a tail of ivy, and my illustrated Rainbow Classics edition of *Wuthering Heights* lay open to an ink drawing of a ghost-girl tugging Mr. Lockwood's arm through a broken window. Interesting choice, Benny said. He spoke louder than necessary, no doubt suing for an audience. Looked around before bending to sit the doll at the foot of my bed. Reached into his back pocket and removed a packet of nuts.

How did he ... ? But he wouldn't let me finish. A little green snake told him, okay? 'Twixt this way, 'twixt that, 'twixt branches, 'twixt blossoms ... *The Golden Flowerpot*, assuming I remembered. In adults the desire to remain innocent frequently takes a perverse form, especially if the adult is drawn to the occult. Meanwhile the oldest and meanest of the nurses marched in with a tray of pleated medicine cups, scowled, and drew the curtains around the bed to my right, where lay the teeny child who'd been mysteriously shrinking ever since she'd been admitted, despite the great heaps of food they shoveled down her throat.

This isn't so bad, Benny said. Is it? How're you doing? He picked up the box and stared through a heart-shaped cellophane window at the little white dress and cap, still attached by wires to its flower-sprigged backdrop. Why don't you open it? he asked, reasonably enough, but I didn't want to explain that in here such questions weren't tolerated, that to open anything was to pin your hopes on a future the gods might decide not to hold in store for you (look what happened to Joy), that this pleasant room was a fraud, a cunningly decorated confection that by night turned to an iced lump of coal, mean old Nurse Root splay-legged in the corner, *Not As a Stranger* (doctors *porking* nurses, said Ravenhair) open on her lap.

We're doing just fine, aren't we? said Nurse Root as from behind the teeny child's curtain came the sound of liquid rattling into a bedpan. Jesus! Ravenhair said, she pisses like a cow.

He had an enchanting way of slipping his tongue into the corner of his mouth and tilting his head to one side when he spoke. The red sun shone all over him. He gave me the stitches from his hernia operation in a small white Baily Banks & Biddle jewelry box as a token of his love.

Meanwhile the same sun was transforming Benny Gold into a beet-red and tedious lout. How stupid he suddenly looked, his rail-thin upper torso draped across the adjustable bedtray, a bead of sweat poised to fall from the tip of his nose! Nor would anyone in the children's ward at Chestnut Hill Hospital dream of suggesting that three fistfuls of lentils, a fistful of cumin, a fistful of string, and the ileum (*guts*, explained Nurse Root with a sigh) of a firstborn animal might cure TB.

Had any visitors? Benny asked casually, and I shook my head. Well, except my parents. Not a—and here, maintaining a slack-lipped and uncharacteristic expression, he gestured: taller than himself, slightly pear-shaped? Nope, I said, and he looked relieved. Some guy named Mink, he explained. About Joy.

But Joy's dead, I said, horrified.

Maybe what happened to Joy wasn't an accident, Benny went on to say. And then Nurse Root was waving an enormous syringe in his face, meaning he should stand off to one side so she could shut the curtain, and when she opened it again he was gone.

The room returned to normal: Teeny whimpering, Ravenhair lecherously looking up the doll's skirt, Nurse Root holding aloft a cylinder filled with blood, on the bedtray a stinking heap of snow-white food. Of course visitors couldn't bear to stay long—we saw to that. Nor was there any question of our condition being accidental. We were shameful, failing test after test, though there was no real evidence beyond the cylinder of blood (never good enough!) and the odd fact of my parents' infrequent visits, both of them (as my father admitted years later) afraid that it was their own doing, having permitted their Rh negative and Rh positive blood to mix in me, despite their being utterly incompatible, even on that most primitive level.

"The best physicians are Doctor Diet and Doctor Quiet and Doctor Merryman," said Mrs. Beeton in an unusually whimsical mood. To which Edwina Moss (in *Home Truths*) added: "You alone must decide which is the less desirable: the gray mice who make their home in your body's walls, or the brindle tom who lays their little organs at its door."

YET HOW COULD BENNY GOLD SAY SUCH a thing? Joy Harbison, my childhood friend, died during Hurricane Hazel, slipped and fell into the creek while walking across the dam at Hermit's Mill, or so everyone thought. Between four and eight p.m., according to Inspector Mink's report, which would put it right around the time we were hiding in the basement. But had she died at the exact moment the willow fell into our backyard, or at some less dramatic moment, when my sister put Noodle in the salmon poacher and he bit her for instance? Or had it been at a moment when nothing at all was happening, my mother fiddling with the Sterno stove, my sister looking off into space, my father sorting screws? She was found in the larger of the two iron pipes called penstocks, protruding from the ruined millworks below Valley Green. Miss Osborne's dog found her.

When your friend dies this is one of the things you try to do, at least at first. You try understanding the death by connecting it to understandable events. You try to get the better of it through ownership. What were *you* doing when it happened? How could you not have known? Through the window the same spray of raindrops flung against the same tree where the same yellow birds are forever about to perch … I have always been with you, says the doll head, meaning the angel of death.

And in the basement a smell that's worse than usual, sulphur, mildew, bleach. Outdoors a yellow slicker faintly visible, stalking through the queer green light. Whatever my mother was cooking on the Sterno stove (meat-cakes? scrambled eggs? Mary Kitchen Roast Beef Hash?) ended up not getting eaten. A snarling sound: my sister began to cry. Like the angel of death the hurricane's eye passed over us. The willow fell. Glass broke. The storm got louder, came inside.

There was no point, never is, in trying to make sense of an accidental death. You creep into bed and hope for sleep. Outside, a world cloaked in fog, the motionless and oddly turbulent atmosphere of a not-yet-discovered planet. First Miss Osborne's dog, then a park guard, then Inspector Mink took over. Benny Gold was questioned, as the last person to have seen Joy alive, though most people seemed to share my grandmother's impatience, her sense that the tragedy was perfectly predictable and that the only mystery was why it had taken so long to happen.

At the corner of Germantown and Willowgrove it wasn't till you were right on top of them that you could see the green mailbox at the curb, the red garden tools in the hardware store window, the wrought-iron balcony where old Mrs. Hardware beat her rugs. The day after Hazel everything was unfamiliar, fog-shrouded, like the artifacts that rose from mist to confound an expert panel of archaeologists on *What in the World?*, my favorite television show of the period. Or maybe it was like a jigsaw puzzle in its earliest stages of completion, when all you see, really, is a gray expanse of tabletop with a queerly shaped clump of leaves here, a knobby piece of blue sky there, an entire(!) red bicycle adrift in the void. For the first time you realize how strange a tree is, how strange a bicycle, how strange the sidewalk fanning around the peculiar round base of the hardware store in enormous pie-wedges.

The concrete was still wet, the wheels of my bike making a torn sound as I steered it over the wedges and onto Willow-grove Avenue, wobbling a little because my sister was perched behind me. You could tell a sun was up there above the swirling mist, and that it was shining, hot even. An invisible trolley advanced, hissed, dinged, hissed, retreated; a nun's wimpled head floated by, a policeman's brass-buttoned chest. Despite parental interdiction we were headed to the Wissahickon: down a steep and dangerous hill (the sidewalk no longer smooth concrete but broken slate) where shrubbed villa metamorphosed into awninged mansion, turreted castle, spired church, then left onto St. Martin's Lane and immediately right onto a mist-shrouded trail that began in shadowy confusion, a tangle of grit-specked weeds and foul smelling sodden trash behind the railroad station, before plummeting straight to the Wissahickon Creek far below.

A Sunday afternoon and, as usual, we were going hiking with Benny Gold, whose day of rest was different from ours. He'd be waiting near historic Valley Green Inn, the image of which my mother was to paint on hundreds (maybe thousands) of lampshades in her lifetime. The windows were cut out so when she turned the light on it shone through the holes. (Unlike the silk shade Christopher Morley's mother adored as a small girl in England, a view of the Wissahickon appearing among "the world's fabled glories.") Let there be light! my mother would say, to which my father would reply, No one's home.

Wissahickon—did it mean "yellow-colored stream" (echoing the raven-haired boy's joke about I. P. Daily)? Or did it mean "catfish creek" (in honor of the three thousand catfish a Mr. Shrunk took from it in a single summer night, as my grandmother claimed while glaring at yet another attempt on my part to braid the lamp tassels in her dark, gloomy, suggestive apartment, the adults drinking manhattans, my sister and I apricot nectar, a popular juice of our childhood that seems since to have disappeared ...). Whatever its name meant, the Wissahickon was the closest thing we had to wilderness in a world otherwise composed of newly poured sidewalks, curbside baby sycamores, lawns like welcome mats, zinnias, marigolds.

Onto the famous Valley Green Bridge and over its crest and then you coasted down down down, through clouds and above the roaring sound of the water. The usual smell of horse manure masked by storm smells: amphibious, dank, thickly glistening. Something untoward had surfaced, though of course I didn't know what, imagined the black moist skin of a dinosaur, an entire dinosaur. I have always been with you, she said. *She*: a girl. But I'm getting ahead of myself.

At Valley Green the Wissahickon widens into a broad cola-colored pool, usually shallow and sun-dappled, now black and swollen by the storm, clogged with debris around which the fly-headed ducks were bobbing, above which the mist hovered and soughed. Somewhere to the south a dog was barking; otherwise the sound of the creek was all you could hear, the clamor of the race below Hermit's Mill. A fallen willow obscured the mounting block Miss Waterbath insisted I use, rather than leap like a desperado onto an already galloping horse. The storm had also yanked the inn's hinged sign from its post, and knocked over most of the porch furniture, including the high-backed rockers in which generally you'd find old ladies sipping tea, surrounded by dutiful progeny, and where I'd sit once my

cursed lesson was over, eating an entire package of Nabisco
Sugar Wafers, while my father chain-smoked Luckys. But today
the porch was empty save for a bullet-headed and freckled
young man in a white kitchen uniform who straddled the rail,
smoking and watching a white-aproned crone inch about on all
fours like a sad crab, sweeping glass shards into a dustpan.

Benny Gold had positioned himself at the root end of the
willow, in the middle of an only slightly diminished group of
disciples. Some people think willows fall, he was saying, because of their shallow root system. But all you have to do is look
at a willow to know it's more water than wood. A many-
branched tree, hence darkly shaded, dangerous. He went on to
explain that willows grew faster than other trees, but also died
sooner. Like water they longed to lie down, making them useless for the construction of everything except baskets. The
Kecks were already there, as well as Patience and Prudence
Teachout, both of whom I suddenly hated as much for their
long goosy necks and dull slack-jawed manner as for the fact
that they weren't Joy, with whom I'd been longing to discuss the
storm.

Where've you been? Benny asked, to which my sister cheer-
fully replied, In jail. Well let's go, he said, and when I asked where
Joy was, he said he thought she'd be with me. I knew I'd already
broken my father's two rules, both unmistakably stamped with
his syntax (You don't want to go letting anyone ride the back of
your bike; you don't want to go crossing the avenue), and was
about to break my mother's (If you touch so much as a twig of
one of those fallen trees you'll end up electrocuted like Mr. Tyre
with the hedge clippers), but I wasn't worried. Having spent all
their energy on the storm, the gods were now bored with our
world and eager to inflict damage elsewhere.

Meanwhile the sound of barking persisted, more or less in the direction of Walnut Lane Bridge. Woof. Woofwoof. Polly Keck was sucking up to Benny in typical fashion, the belted canteen riding low on her hips like a ceinture on an odalisque. A light breeze was blowing, shaking huge drops of water from the tulip trees, the hemlocks. I just can't figure out why you aren't a teacher, Polly Keck was saying. You're a hundred times smarter than Mr. Chodorkoff. Woofwoof. Woof. Woofwoofwoof. I just can't figure out why you're a moron, Henry Keck said, and Prudence Teachout laughed nastily. Benny said nothing, preferring to let us fight our own battles.

A heavy woman on a palomino—Miss Waterbath on Serenade? it was so hard to recognize anyone—parted the curtains of mist, cantered past, let the curtains fall shut behind her. But where *was* Joy, a little like a palomino herself, beige face, yellow hair? On our right the public fountain (Esto Perpetua), its water running clear as crystal; on our left the Wissahickon, brackish and darkly furrowed, swarming with perch fry, scraps of algae, flanks and arching necks of water, mica-flecked, foam-specked, muscular and tense.

Phineas Soames, the rector of St. Martin-in-the-Fields, approached, Miss Osborne, the aging deaconess, leaning on his arm. How do you do, ladies? Miss Osborne said. We are fine, thank you, said Henry Keck, falsetto. Perhaps you can help, Miss Osborne continued, undaunted. I seem to have lost my pup. She plucked at the rector's sleeve and he paused, unreeling a pocket watch on a preposterously long gold chain. He was a big rawboned man, though his face was smooth and unlined, babyish even. But did it mirror the untroubled waters of a faithful heart, or was he too, as Henry Keck insisted, a moron? (Why did Soames tiptoe past the medicine cabinet?) Don't for-

get I'm to see Dr. Dick about his organ at five, Reverend
Soames said, and Henry elbowed Patience Teachout, who stared
at him blankly. Everyone knew he had a crush on her, though
obviously nothing would ever come of it. Miss Osborne was
staring at Benny, a shadow of hurt and impatience darkening
her eyes, as if he were late for a tryst. And why suddenly look to
a man for answers, having done without for sixty-some-odd
years?

The sound of barking started up again, closer than before. Ah, Rusty! said Miss Osborne. Rusty? Rusty! Gray movement in the gray mist: a big gray dog, its fur coming loose in
patches like carpet samples. Prudence Teachout picked up the
stick it dropped at her feet, threw it expertly with a flick of the
wrist, and quick as a wink the dog was back, pouncing flat on its
forelegs, dropping the stick and barking, its ass in the air, its tail
wildly wagging. Shoo! Prudence said. Shoo! The dog's breath
stank, its eyes were rheumy, its teeth yellow. Only a week ago
someone saw a rabid squirrel in Manayunk—could that be a
fleck of foam on Rusty's muzzle? How ironic to die of rabies
just when the whole world had turned to water!

Gimme that, said Henry, grabbing, but Prudence whirled
away; for someone who looked so dopey she was surprisingly
fleet. She hurled the stick with all the force she could muster
and, amazingly, instead of watching it vanish into the haze, we
suddenly found ourselves able to follow its golden flight,
twirling higher and higher like a majorette's baton before coming to rest in the shining upheaval at the base of the dam. Fetch
that I dare thee! Patience hollered.

Sunlight pouring through the tulip leaves, the crowns of
the hemlocks. On the gray tabletop among the puzzle pieces a
red stain, a yellow eye, a black hightop—many things previously

hidden were preparing to reveal themselves with terrible clarity. Rusty clambered down the bank, began racing back and forth, stopping intermittently to paw the dirt, his sharp barks decaying into small throaty whines. The faintest flicker of movement: a green worm dangling like a fishhook in midair; a red salamander hiding like a jujube under a leaf. One minute Benny was standing there with us on the path, tugging off his shoes, the next he was wading into the creek. Everything clear, like a strand of hair that's gotten caught in your mouth, that has somehow managed to lodge itself between two molars. How repulsive, the thin squeal of hair against enamel, the sensation of the teeth gripping it, jarred at the root with each tug. In my pocket I found the bubblegum fortune Joy had given me only the day before yesterday; the salamander prepared to speak. "Death is the wages of inattention," said Bazooka Joe, unless I've got it wrong and that was the salamander, making it Joe who said, "A fowl weather friend ain't no chicken."

The sun released the sweet smells of leaf mold and decomposition from the Wissahickon's branch-shadowed, light-dappled paths; of frog spawn from its diamond-shot, sun-braided creek. Suddenly there were people everywhere, flashily dressed, in a holiday mood. Had they been there all along, mute as giraffes? Holy shit, said Henry Keck, wiping his nose on the sleeve of his filthy blue-and-white-striped jersey.

Is it possible for the body to be inhabited by a force so strong it no longer knows who it is, what it is saying? You might just as well open your jaws and ask God to yank free your soul. Remember that your body is merely a temporary dwelling, on loan to you for the Lord to use as he wishes.

A foot in a black hightop was sticking out of the penstock. Joy Harbison's foot, Joy Harbison lying there on her back in an inch or so of rank water, her yellow eyes wide open, a thread of blood dangling from the corner of her mouth, her neck broken at the sixth cervical vertebra, seat of self-deceit and inspiration. A large gray dog looked in at her, its front paws braced on the penstock's rust-stained iron rim; it stood there, barking and barking, louder and louder, the barks rebounding like bullets off the iron walls, filling the space inside with an increasingly thick tube of sound. But it hardly mattered how loud the sound was, for who could hear it, contained as it was within the walls of that heavy iron pipe, the pipe itself within a roaring wall of water?

WHEN A LITTLE GIRL IS GIVEN A DOLL, she's given a lifeless thing of which she believes herself to be the mother. Because the doll is her daughter (even if it's "grown-up" and the games she plays with it are elaborate, sophisticated, Little Women, Wuthering Heights, the wind and the rain and, if the head unscrews, French Revolution …) the little girl senses herself and the doll to be of the same composition, like a real mother and her daughter.

Freud touched on this subject in his famous essay on the uncanny. It's a subject that also fascinated E. T. A. Hoffmann, whose story "The Sandman" Freud took for his central example. But a man always thinks of his child as a thing apart from himself, despite being invested or even filled like a beaker with his qualities. On some level a man always experiences his child as a mystery, whereas for a woman, because the daughter forms in the crucible of herself, it's as if a piece of her sloughs off, like a calving glacier. A mystery? Yes, but no more so than she is. *Life* is the accident. That is what a young girl knows when she is given a doll.

So she lies there in the dark hospital.

Everyone has gone home and she's all alone, experiencing that most extreme form of solitude, to be awake among sleepers. Across the room Ravenhair breathes softly like a fairy princess; off to her right Teeny snores like a drunk geezer. But what on earth is the source of that uncanny light shining in the Flemish doll's eyes? Is it coming from the hall? Lit from within? Or did Benny Gold exchange his own eyes for the doll's, the way the Fates pass around their single gray eyeball?

And what about the Sandman, whom the young girl has always considered (besides that hyperactive salt mill) one of her father's most horrific inventions? According to Hoffmann he's a wicked man who comes to little children when they won't go to bed and throws handfuls of sand in their eyes, so that they jump out of their heads all bloody; then he puts the eyes into a sack and carries them off to the half-moon as food for his own little ones; and they sit up in the nest and have hooked beaks like owls, which they use to peck out the eyes of naughty little boys and girls.

THE MOUSE IS CROUCHED IN THE LIVING room corner, watching the dead girl make her difficult ascent of the dresser's north face, hauling herself from drawer pull to drawer pull and across the wooden lawn to arrive gasping on the blue square of carpet sample. The father gives her a comradely poke because he's relieved to see a familiar face, even though she doesn't seem to have a clue who he is. In any case his heart goes out to her, she's such an ugly little creature.

Shall we dance? the father asks. Shall we fly? Under the circumstances I'm sure Dorothy won't raise any objections. As for Gold, I'm sorry to have to be the one to break it to you, but he's strictly a one-man operation, like that showboat in the gutter with the umbrella, you know the one. George. George Kelly.

Gene, the mouse corrects.

Him, the father concedes. I saw him dancing around out there in the pouring rain like an idiot. Don't get me wrong, I'm not afraid of dying. Gold's the one who's afraid of dying. Gold's the one with all the plans up his sleeve. Why don't we just leave him there like that for a while? Maybe he'll learn a little humility.

The father sighs, whistles, gestures with his thumb, but weakly, weakly. It's been days since he's eaten, though he seems to remember sipping apple juice through a bent straw. Or maybe not days, but years. A long time ago, that much is clear, back when his mouth was dry and sticky, and he wanted his teeth brushed constantly to make sure that wherever he was going (and he *was* going somewhere) his breath at least was fresh. The habits we form during life determine the way we prepare to leave it. Lying there on his back, on the chain of his spine, each vertebra numbered. T-2, the second bone in the thoracic region, threaded through like a button with nerves leading to the heart. He could feel the angel of death (female, natch) tugging at it and he wanted to be fresh-mouthed, ready to kiss ...

Hey! says the dead girl. Knock it off. But the father's in no mood for rejection. What difference can it make? he asks, reasonably enough. We're ghosts. He points the girl toward the mirror. Have a look, he says, but he can't hear her answer because, all at once, she's screaming.

It is late afternoon. A red sun deepens the gloss of the mouse's plump gray body, shines through its ears, crisscrossed with delicate veins. Ghosts? the mouse says, dismissive. It has moved most of the furniture out of the living room, dumping one sofa on the floor and hauling the other, as well as the parrot stand, gramophone, wheeled tea cart, three split peas, and a dark orange scrap of American cheese, onto the dropping-specked dresser scarf. Not ghosts, it says, twitching its moist black nose. You mean perhaps *food*?

Given a choice between it and the father, the girl finds herself gravitating toward the mouse, so beautiful despite the needle-sharp teeth, the pin-bright eyes. Nor does the mouse seem to expect anything from her. On the contrary, it appears to find her repulsive. No one's going to want to eat you, it explains. No offense, but you smell spoiled.

No offense taken. The girl backs off to one side where she can see a big human eye peeking in through the hall window. Is that more to your liking? she asks. Though isn't it true that mice live crowded together in filthy holes, that they'll eat anything, and are carriers of typhoid, spotted fever, plague? Of course she can't smell a thing, not having a nose herself, so even were she to have an offensive odor, she'd be the last to know. And as for ghosts and food?—she has to admit that the connection eludes her.

Of course it does, the mouse replies, oh-so-patient. That's because *you're* dead when you're eaten. By the time the worms eat *you*, you've been dead for a while, and they can look high and low but they're not going to find your spirit. That's because your spirit's fled, to where, who knows? Not my problem. Whereas we're still alive and kicking on our way down the cat's throat. Down the throat and into the stomach and there we stay. You can either be a ghost or you can be food. You can't be both.

So you don't think we have souls? the girl asks. She sounds crestfallen.

Is that what I said? No. I never said that. Everyone knows there are five types, including wormfodder, the lowest of the low, type five.

It's a windless day filled with the smell of cut grass and bleach. From nearby comes a little whine and the sound of toenails scratching on wood; a shiver runs through the mouse's sleek gray body. But how warm the sun, how unbearably fragrant the air, how poignant the sight of old Joe's and young Joey's boxers stiffening on the line! That would be you, the mouse continues, measuring the distance from the dresser to its hole in the back of the closet. Type five. Any minute now, it knows, that infernal dachshund will come bursting through the door ...

OUTSIDE THE SUN HAS RISEN HIGH ABOVE the arbor, revealing the hideous tents of the gypsy moths, their sudden appearance among the fruit as troubling to Edwina's sense of propriety as the sight of Gertie, darkly blurred and remote, in her own gauze cocoon. Both going about their business secretly, though Gertie at least doesn't seem to have been wrapped by an insane nurse in pileous gray bandages, similar to the one wreathing poor Henny's thumb.

Pook, Edwina says. Come. She draws on her wrapper and steps into her deerskin slippers. There are advantages to staying inside a tent, she remarks, and Pook wags his tail, happy to be addressed by his beloved. But you don't think about such things, do you? Being so open-natured and pure of heart. You, with your big smiling face. You don't care who sees what *you're* doing. A soft little noise comes from within Gertie's tent, a delicate rustling like mice in the walls, breeze in the pines. It must be getting late, Edwina decides, even though wisps of fog are still coming detached from Egg Pond, pure white and spindle-shaped, unreeling into a sky that lacks color yet is vivid, as if the fog sets standards of whiteness impossible to match.

And then she notices that the doctor has left his bag on Gertie's dresser. An excuse to return? Or merely absentminded, the way he ambled off one day to visit relations in White River and ended up at Harvard Medical School, evidently preferring the company of cadavers to her own. In a woman love goes from the soul to the senses and often fails to reach them, while in a man it goes the other way around, likewise missing the mark. A doctor's bag isn't so private as a lady's purse, Edwina reasons, unbuckling the strap, but when she looks inside she's shocked to find a bundle of tracts and a sack heavy with coins. *THE MIRACLE OF GERTRUDE MOSS, being the true story of the Fasting Girl of Moss Cottage as told by her Physician, Simon Wingfield, M.D., 10 cents.* The Fasting Girl has mystic powers, according to the tract. She requires no food, is clairvoyant, etc. etc. She's an angel, hasn't taken a bite since the day she was born, nourishes herself on light and air. No night soil, the tract boasts, if one needs more evidence of the Miraculous come to reside in a humble northern village.

This would serve to explain the unusual flurry of activity Edwina realizes she's been aware of for some time now in the house (doors banging, windows opening, random coughs and sneezes), as well as the odd assortment of objects on Gertie's dresser (an angel in a blown-glass paperweight, a stuffed bird, a canning jar crammed with daisies). Gifts from credulous admirers, no doubt, at least one of whom has left behind a trail of muddy footprints. And while the paperweight's quite beautiful, the bird is clearly the work of an amateur, poignant, like the daisies, both of them crawling with bugs.

Let's see what your master has to say about this, Edwina mutters, holding up the sack and jingling it menacingly as they make their way downstairs, past the elegantly appointed rooms of the second floor. Someone is stirring in the Ivy Room, noisily clearing his throat; in the Peacock Room the springs of the Chinese bed sing, there's a hushed slithering sound, and Edwina thinks she can hear a woman attempting to stifle a cry. Soon they will all be up, the lot of them, wanting breakfast. A cold joint nicely garnished, poached eggs, muffins. The cut-glass bowl filled with fresh strawberries. Devil on Horseback, that old standby, prunes wrapped in bacon and skewered to a piece of toast. But which is the devil and which is the horse? And isn't it possible that she's mistaken, that the rooms are completely empty? It's an old house, after all, and in summer the wood expands, creaking and moaning. Your master put his finger on it, Edwina tells Pook (who always appears to be smiling at her indulgently when he pants). I am losing my mind, a loss for which some, sad to say, might give thanks.

Her plan has been to oversee breakfast preparations, then head immediately to the courtyard, where the men will be testing the horses' girths, checking the hooves for pebbles one last time. But the minute she arrives in the downstairs hall Pook lets out a loud bark and tears off through the dining room, coming to a halt in front of the door to her study, where he begins growling ominously, a resonant growl from deep within his mammoth rib cage that rattles the windows.

In the dining room, sun shines brightly, lighting the top of the mahogany table, the best Limoges china smeared with egg yolk and dotted with crumbs. A setting for how many? Five? Six? The courtyard seems vacant, though there are signs of recent occupation, the lettuce trampled, one of the bean tepees atilt, several steaming piles of manure among the blood-red spines of the chard. How can the world's skin be so infinitely permeable when Gertie's is not? Is it because to be alive is to resist assault? And only when you are dead can you be planted, even the most durable parts of you finally giving way, worms in, worms out, everything channeled through those mindless digestive systems until you too are dirt, though whatever has sprouted and flowered in the process cannot be seen or held or nurtured, unlike what happens when you plant a seed.

Edwina sits at the table and cradles her head in her hands. Everything is wrong, and has never been otherwise. She picks up a partly eaten triangle of toast and takes a bite. While her daughter starves herself in the night nursery, her husband will be skewering himself like a prune on a Rebel bayonet. Everything is wrong, she is a failure, a bad wife, a catastrophic mother, a wretched hostess. Even Pook seems suddenly thriftless, his coat dull, his eyes glassy and red-rimmed, and when she catches sight of her face in the mirror over the sideboard, she knows it must have been a woman who came up with the idea of Medusa.

To the west the sun exposes the valley, draining by slow degrees down the side of it, filling it with white morning light. It's going to be very hot, of that much Edwina is certain. The crowns of the maples on the other side of Egg Pond have turned from dark-green smudges to bottle-green leaf clusters; a gleaming thread of road appears, and on it blue-uniformed men, galloping faster and faster in the direction of the capital. Idly she lifts another scrap of toast and begins mopping up egg yolk. Someone (Emerson Collier, her otherwise meticulous editor?) has been smoking a cigar, leaving a rain of ash across the table.

But where's Henny? The room's a mess, the birds have finished their morning songs, the clock is striking the half hour, the day's well under way. Time to singe and draw the ducks before they go bad. Time to get moving.

Edwina sighs, wipes her mouth on the back of her hand like a yokel. Pookie, she says, her voice sharp, for once again the dog is behaving in a disturbing manner, prancing stiff-legged back and forth at the study door, letting out a resonant growl, pausing to cock his head, first to one side, then the other, just as he listens to snowbanks for the sounds of tunneling voles.

Get back, Edwina says sharply, and Pook creeps under the table, still growling, sets the huge pumpkin of his head on his paws, and gloomily regards the dust motes dancing in the sun. Though he can't say it (dogs, thank God, unable to mimic the human voice), clearly Pook knows she needs his protection, just as he doesn't intend to remain under the table. He thumps his thick burdock-matted tail, once, twice, against the central pedestal, and when Edwina bends to reassure him, he licks her cheek. More often than not the worlds of dog and spirit intersect, a fact of which his poor mistress, so very sad today, so very very sad, is completely unaware. Human kisses, dry and round; delicious human breath! But there are things in this world from which even your dog can't protect you ...

Within the study the drapes have been drawn, leaving the room cool and dark. Even so, Edwina immediately realizes that it's full of people, including the delinquent Henny, boldly perched on her mistress's English lounge chair, fanning her wings among its cabbage roses like a moth come to rest in a giant's garden. How have so many people managed to cram themselves into so small a space? That's definitely Miss MacConchie lounging in the window seat, the gypsy's hissing basket in her green satin lap, but she's surrounded by several women and girls Edwina only vaguely recognizes (that lumpish yellow-haired creature, for one), all of them wearing the crude shortgowns and aprons of the Poor Farm. Passing around a teacup filled with opium-laced wine, gloomily singing: "Heaven her gates unbars, flinging her increase of light ... Guard us from harm without, cleanse us from evil within ..." And, yes, there's Emerson Collier (who must have crept into the house while Edwina slept) paging through *The Blancmange*, his lips pursed skeptically, his eyes set in his brow like raisins in a Bath bun. Or at least Edwina thinks it's her manuscript he's reading, since her view's partly blocked by the commanding figure of a man, his long graying hair gathered at the nape of his neck in a twist of fabric. Simon Wingfield, she guesses, the fraud.

Cautiously she moves farther into the room to get a better look. It *is* Simon Wingfield, the usual severity of his expression having assumed a peculiar molten quality, a hint of weakness he makes no attempt to hide, luring Edwina closer and closer like one of the luckless citizens of Pompeii. She feels her face burn, though no one seems to notice. What's that? she whispers, watching as he attaches a crank-handled metal drum by a length of wire to a beaker, and Henny, the expert, whispers back. A Leyden jar, ma'am. It gives you a jolt. She twitches her arms and legs, bugs her eyes. It makes you dance, she adds, and begins to laugh nervously, until the yellow-haired girl thumps her on the back. Please, Emerson Collier complains.

Meanwhile Simon Wingfield bends over the drum, holding a square of cloth to its surface as he energetically turns the crank. His gray horsetail whips from side to side; his thin lips are set in a frown. Was he lying when he excoriated the Spiritualists? Maybe he's a spy, a bad apple planted among good and intended to corrupt, though he seems serious enough. Electricity, he explains. The static electricity produced by rubbing felt against metal is now being channeled through the wire and into the beaker, causing sparks to dance on his hand, hissing and popping, not unlike what happens when you run your fingers the wrong way through a cat's fur.

Their method, he tells Edwina, is simple. They sit in a circle and pass around the beaker. Slowly at first, then faster and faster until the light becomes a blur, a lit doorway into the present, a kind of beacon for the wandering souls of the dead. I know how very difficult this must be for you, he says, but it's good that you've finally decided to join us. There's something suspect in his voice, a solicitous note that sends a shiver down Edwina's spine. Or perhaps it's the room, oddly chill with the curtains drawn. Even the doctor shudders when he hands the jar to Henny.

Gertrude Moss, she says, lifting her face like a dark flower in the time-honored pose of the female ecstatic (though there can be no denying that her teeth are bad, her breath malodorous). Gertrude Moss, can you hear me? But how could I have been such a dunce? Edwina wonders. Of course Gertie's the one he wants. He's merely turning spiritualism to his own advantage, just as he did with me. And then all at once the implications of his scheme begin to dawn on her, and she's weak with horror. Let me go, she says, feeling the tears press from between her lashes, but Miss MacConchie has risen to block the door. Gertie, Henny begs. Gertrude Moss! Where you off to, child? The room's not only chill but thick with a faintly sweet yet repulsive smell, redolent of deer rotting in the woods, milk burned on a stove lid.

Meanwhile Pook has crept into the corner where he appears to be sniffing noisily, rudely, at Henny's feet, or at least in the vicinity of her feet—it's so difficult to see anything! Indeed all you can see is the glowing beaker, and the lit eyeballs of the Spiritualists. Stop it, Henny orders, though there seems to be something wrong with her voice, almost as if she's the source of the smell, as if her voicebox is decaying, turning to mush. And why must Pook keep up that odious lapping, that infernal snuffling . . .

This is absurd! Edwina shouts. What do you think you're doing? For your information my daughter's right where I left her, sound asleep in her bedroom. And even were she not, even God forbid were she no longer in the land of the living, the immortal soul of Gertie Moss would never be tempted back to earth by a bunch of fools and a lit beaker. Do you hear me? Never!

Calm yourself, my dear, says Miss MacConchie. Hush, hush. Her own father, she explains, was called back from death's door by the sound of his beloved daughter's knitting needles clicking several inches from his comatose head. And when he awakened, there was a hat! Two birds with one stone, that's the way it is with a miracle, Miss MacConchie exults. It always has its feet planted firmly in both worlds.

Edwina realizes she's crying, and Simon Wingfield has his arm around her. He's dabbing at her tears with a length of flannel bandage, murmuring *darling*, but she shakes him off. My husband will be here any minute, she admonishes, and notices the Poor Farm girls exchange a look. Don't go pitying *me*, she snarls, still weeping. You're the ones who are barking up the wrong tree, looking for ghosts here in Moss Cottage, of all places. Everyone knows that a haunted house suffers from an abundance of spirit.

Please, Mrs. Moss, the yellow-haired girl says. It's not so bad as you think. Your girl can talk to us and you can too. She hands her the glowing beaker and Edwina feels a jolt, feels hot breezes rattling the ash boughs of her ribs, a fist slamming upward from her stomach, its mission to crack open the skull and let out the brain . . .

. . .

Midsummer, a clearing. Edwina's young husband is felling an oak. Over and over the axe bites through the furrowed bark, revealing the tender wood beneath, as beautiful and smooth as his infant daughter's skin. Too beautiful to waste on a table, he decides. A cradle? But Gertie's growing so rapidly, and besides, her mother insists babies sleep better in nests of ladyfern and moss. Headstrong yet generally right, Edwina. He can just make out her broad muscular back there where he left her picking bergamot on the other side of the millrace, far enough away to be safe, but close enough to hear the wrenched, groaning sound the tree will make as it breaks in two. Bees hover above the bergamot's spiky red flowers, above its rumpled leaves which, when steeped in boiling water, release a smell of spice, of distant lands.

Meanwhile Gertie's lying flat on her back in her soft, fragrant nest with her eyes wide open, staring at clouds, filmy, fibrous clouds similar to the caul she was born with, as they slip past overhead. Surrounded by horsetails (*Equisetum arvense*, also called pot-scrubber, common to waste places and wetlands), heralding a change of weather. When the oak hits the clearing floor, the earth leaps under her body; it's as if she's been asleep ever since she was born and has finally awakened. Bright drops of rain tumble through the air, beading on the moss; horsetails above, horsetails below. Horsetails poking up all around her, translucent, flesh-hued tubes marked at intervals with small black knobs, each stem crowned with a larger black knob, spindle-shaped, queerly pocked and crimpled, like something wadded in a pocket which once removed and shaken loose becomes immense ...

Soon her papa will begin planing the wood, cutting it into planks, then pegging them together into a chest; two sides, the

back and lid, he'll polish with beeswax but leave otherwise un-
ornamented, the better to display the honey color of the wood,
the fine whorls of its grain. The front, on the other hand, he'll
divide into panels of varying size stained the color of almond
skin, thirty-four of them horizontal, three vertical, a pattern accented by the paler framework. In ten of the twelve smallest
panels gemlike buttons painted black, their arrangement across
the surface undulant, a valley between hills; in each of the three
vertical panels a more intricately turned trio, also black, the
flanking pair simple amphorae, as if to call attention to the central figure, its disturbing symmetry not unlike the horsetails',
perversely mutable, swelling and narrowing, swelling and narrowing, the dark germ out of which life first seeps, the dark hole
into which it finally drains.

    In one of the remaining panels, a black G, in the other, an M.

    And coming from inside, a little girl's voice. Let me out!
Let me out! Let me out!

WHEN THE KNOCK COMES THEY'RE AT the molded lead table, a group nowhere near as illustrious as that gathered around the table at Malmaison or in the house of God, yet every bit as crowded together. Clockwise, from the seat nearest the kitchen door, the mother, the grandfather, the grandmother, the father, the younger daughter. (A circle, the hardest thing to get yourself out of, especially once you've joined hands to say grace.) How can you permit such filth near your food? the grandmother asks the mother, ostensibly referring to the parrot clumsily Scotch-taped to the parrot stand and the gray plastic dachshund under the table, though everyone knows she means the father. When the knock comes, he's just inserted and lit an incense "cigarette" in a hole expressly designed for that purpose in the dog's mouth, filling the room with puffs of queer-smelling smoke. Think of the poor child's lungs if nothing else, the grandmother says, meaning the older daughter, who has only today been released from the tubercular colony (high in the Alps on the shelf above the maple bed), this being a Welcome Home party. And where's the guest of honor? you might ask. Upstairs in the night nursery, the crocheted bedspread pulled over her unnaturally white face, her cheeks highlighted with bright red (Coty's Desiree) nail polish.

Not all the guests are people. Tonight, for example, the grandfather's a wooden clothespin, his wife the little French-woman painted on the Quimper bud vase. Meanwhile the fa-ther, pointer as usual, is hop-hop-hopping down the stairs on one foot (i.e. fingertip) to see who's there. If you sit that way you'll get a hump, says the grandmother to the younger daugh-ter. Only a starving Armenian slurps his food like that, she says. Refined little ladies and gentlemen sit up straight and are quiet as mice.

A fire of balsam fir burns fitfully in the fireplace which, since it's no longer needed at the tubercular colony, is now posi-tioned against the rear wall of the dining room in such a way as to cover the adhesive-taped wire. Balsam fir, its message the same as that stitched on the pine-and-fir-stuffed pincushion Joy brought back from the Poconos. I PINE FOR YOU AND THEN I BALSAM. The meat-cakes are a little tough, n'est-ce pas, Dotty dear? You must watch that Joe Caruso like a hawk or you'll get a stone when you've asked for sirloin, the grandmother says, at which the grandfather laughs and says *You're* the tough cookie, and the grandmother's upper lip begins to tremble.

Of course it's impossible, as Edwina Moss herself was well aware, to play hostess to an unruly group of guests when you are distracted. The clock strikes, the shadows lengthen. The guests are all famished, playing with their utensils, shredding bread, shaking salt onto the tabletop and drawing pictures in it with their fingers. No matter that your world is falling apart; your guests are bored by your problems except insofar as they interfere with dinner.

It seems hours have passed since Edwina first noticed rain pattering through her open window. If she doesn't do some-thing immediately those wretched ducks (dangling from the

same hook where the gypsy's basket used to hang) will be ruined, their blood glutinous, putrid. How fatiguing can seem
one's obligation to appetite; how preferable Gertie's solution!
Nor does Gertie lack for companionship, since when you dine
on air, you dine with the dead. Edwina stirs up the coals, then
begins to stuff the ducks with sage and garlic, salt and pepper.
From the dining room comes the sound of stamping, followed
by a vague shuffling noise, lax yet oddly precise, as if an approaching mummy's trying very hard not to trip over its own
unraveling feet.

A watched pot never boils, Edwina remarks, though need-
less to say the guests can't hear her, having grown quarrelsome
and noisy—why won't they hold their tongues? Perhaps if she
were to deny them light and air, like endive, the color would
drain from their bodies and they'd disappear completely. She
tests the temperature of the sauté pan—perfect!—and then the
stimulating hiss of flesh. The ducks are so small they'll be done
in a trice, but first she must brown them beautifully all over, the
darlings.

Averting her face, she pours in a goblet of port; there's an
explosion of boiling liquid, steam rising in a stinging hot cloud,
and then, once the lid's in place, nothing. When heated, muscle
shrinks and tenses. The fibers wring themselves together as a
laundrymaid wrings a wet shirt, a frustrated suitor his hands, a
broken heart its strings. Everything edible, once it has passed
under the hands of the cook, assumes new forms.

But now they're suddenly all attention! the father having
hopped back up the stairs, bringing with him Inspector Gilbert
Mink, the spitting image of the butler despite the sopping London Fog trench coat. I apologize for interrupting your supper,

he says, and as he stands there dripping on the rug the grandmother remarks that it's just as well, the meat was inedible,
though that's still no excuse for bad manners. Madam, forgive
me, the inspector replies, a thousand pardons. Nonetheless he
seems utterly unapologetic, and when the father causes one of
the pale blue kitchen chairs to levitate and land in the space between the grandfather and grandmother, suggesting that he
might like to take a load off and join them in a meat-cake, the
inspector doesn't hesitate. Or at least he "sits" (stiff as a poker),
while refusing the meat-cake, since he hasn't the faintest idea
what one is.

I hope you realize I wouldn't have bothered you if it
weren't important, says Inspector Mink mysteriously. He fishes
a notepad from one of his trench coat's many pockets, then
slides a pencil from behind his ear and licks its tip, a habit the
grandmother will be the first to tell him is both uncouth and
deadly. A puzzling family, he thinks, for if their education and
social status (not to mention their expensive mahogany furniture) are as superior to his own as seems to be the case, then
what're they doing living here on the wrong side of the tracks in
a house the size of a shoebox? Despite the woman's accent they
must be upstarts, he concludes, and suddenly no longer feels
slow-moving and dull, but robust and savvy, ready for anything.
It's just that new information has come to light, the inspector
continues, though I'm not yet at liberty to reveal . . .

But thank God at last they're to have some games! A
player will secretly think of a person or thing, and the other
players will "guess" what it is, though in the absence of any
hints or clues their answers will be mere shots in the dark. What
Is My Thought Like: a typical nineteenth-century game, perverse and pointless. The clock strikes and Henny shuffles off

with the empty tray. The yellow-haired girl is "it"; to mimic concentration she slides her eyelids over her tiny eyes, her hulkishness becoming suddenly impressive, orphic.

A lump of chalk, says Miss MacConchie; Cleopatra, says one of the Poor Farm girls; a gooseberry, says a second; a shuttlecock, says a third. *The Blancmange*, sneers Emerson Collier. Invited to join, Simon Wingfield declines, claiming an unfair advantage. Suddenly the rain, which seemed to have let up, begins again, harder than before, pounding against the windows, turning the garden to mud, releasing the smell of mud and sending it into the room. I was thinking of Joy, the yellow-haired girl reveals, poor little Joy Harbison, wherever she may roam, and now the game becomes more intriguing as the players attempt to justify their otherwise meaningless answers with similes. (Why is Joy Harbison like a lump of chalk, Cleopatra, a gooseberry? Because she is so very pale, because she harbors a snake in her bosom, because she is a perfect fool, etc. etc.)

... new evidence, Inspector Mink concludes. Pertinent to our investigation of Miss Harbison's death. I *said* foul play, the grandmother crows, didn't I? Didn't I? But the grandfather's attention is fixed on the wall-less side of the room, where the older daughter in her flowered kimono (stolen from the doll Marie-Thé-Lambert, quite the world traveler, sent back to the mother from Japan) is making her shaky way down the invisible attic staircase. What can you tell me about a Mr. Benjamin Franklin Gold? asks Inspector Mink, poised to write, his eyes flashing. How long have you known him? When did you last see him?

Benjamin Franklin? says the younger daughter. He was struck by lightning. He went to sea, silver buckles on his knee. She holds to her mouth the pair of red wax lips the father brought back from Atlantic City. I can wear these or I can eat them, she says, and when the grandmother makes a truly grue-some face at her she bursts into tears. Excuse me? the inspector asks, and the mother says, Time for bed, dah-ling, it's a school day tomorrow. My daughter's right, the father adds pleasantly, Gold, who is, incidentally, a jackass, shipped out a week ago for parts unknown. And by the same token, correct me if I'm wrong, but isn't tomorrow Sunday?

Pouring rain and the occasional flash of lightning, brief rumble of thunder, though thank God we've gotten past the night when the dead walk, when I waited, breathless, terrified, for the sound of Joy's tread on the stairs, having wished and then not-wished then wished again ("he felt his way round the table, and groped along the wall until he found himself in the small passage with the unwholesome paw in his hand ...") to see her once more.

Look who decided to grace us with her presence. Well well well, if it isn't Sleeping Beauty. Are we keeping you up? And so forth, in that vein. Water dripping from the lank forelock of the stranger sitting in my chair and onto the mahogany table-top, and how can this be allowed to happen, since moisture rings are one of my mother's worst nightmares? When you come as I do from a long line of furniture, and not a stick of it without its own name (bachelor chest, piecrust table, Queen Anne highboy, grandfather clock), you know that to scar even the lowliest end table is to hurt a beloved relative. Silent butler, Joy would say, swinging open the lid. Peel me a grape, Jeeves. The stuff in here's always the same. Do you still even *have* this puzzle?, holding up a crescent-shaped piece of parrot beak.

You're the one I was hoping to talk to, says the stranger. Rosamund MacConchie said you and Miss Harbison were the best of friends, is that correct?

I guess so. (Diffident and mournful, thinking of the pantry at Ashgrove, Joy slumped open-mouthed across the countertop like a swimmer momentarily resting on a raft, her hake-pale arms laid out palm down, Miss MacConchie attempting to coil her yellow braids into the little knobs over each ear that she called "snails." Tugging harder than necessary, no doubt angry because she'd just ruined her dentures biting into the grape Joy failed to mention was frozen solid. Rosamund, who'd ever have guessed? Nearby something weird, as usual, draining through cheesecloth into a beige-and-brown-striped bowl.) Maybe not *best*, I say, to cover my traces, at which my sister yells Worst! Worst of friends!, my clacking grandfather takes her onto his lap, my mother remarks that I've been unwell, and the inspector cocks an eyebrow. I'm sorry, he says, of course it's traumatic to lose a friend, and then because this suggestion of mental instability's more than my mother can bear, at last I get to hear, though a hissed whisper, exactly what was wrong with me.

Can I interest you in a cup of coffee? my father asks. A slice of Dorothy's homemade apple pie?

Well, not blood sisters, I say, watching the inspector pick at the woven placemat, his long slender fingers unweaving it, as if to trick me into thinking he's no longer interested in taking notes. But we spent a lot of time together, I add, and he nods yes to the coffee and pie, as well as to egg me on. Would it be safe to say that the two of you spent a good deal of time in the company of Mr. Benjamin Gold?

Uh-huh. Also Henry and Polly Keck, Jamie O'Rourke. It was like a club, you know, in the Wissahickon. Nope, no clubhouse, only a cave. The Teachouts. Joy knew him first. (And was so crazy about him she frequently pretended indifference though I leave that part out, oh yes I do, Joy! remaining faithful to the end, to the memory of a girl stumping along ahead of me across a silent and shadowy ridge high above the creek, snails on her ears, clad in the red playsuit she adored though it brought out the yellowish cast of her skin, showed off the mosquito bites on her midriff she'd scratch till they oozed. We're *law-ust*, she was saying, singsongy and censorious, as if it were my fault. A touch of something like what? complicity? a weird mix of smarminess and irony? thrown in. I confess, sometimes I really couldn't stand her, but I never wished her dead ... And so we stumped along, pretending not to want to catch up, hearing Benny's voice around the next bend, hup hup hup, Polly Keck's phony tinkling laugh. Hello girls, he said, clearly pleased to have led us into a part of the Wissahickon we'd never seen before, darker if possible, certainly moister, a springhead of black water pumping in jerks from the foot of a large trapezoidal hole, the entrance to the cave of the insane hermit who burrowed it out himself, thus giving the nearby suburb of Roxborough its name. "Without, the night was cold and wet, but in the small parlor of Lakesnam Villa the blinds were drawn and the fire burned brightly ..." A chewed sugar doughnut atop the commemorative marker erected by the Rosacrucians, "and the dirty shriveled little paw"—put that down, Henry!—"pitched on the sideboard with a carelessness which betokened no great belief in its virtues ...")

The inspector's expression has changed from avid to wary. As far as you know, he asks, did Joy ever go to the cave with him alone? This would be Hermit Cave you're referring to, am I right, near Hermit's Mill? Prodding the piecrust with his fork, then stabbing it, for my mother's fabled genius with pastry has fallen on hard times of late. I shiver, draw my flowered robe tighter around me, say I don't think so. What're you driving at?

my father asks. What new evidence? And just to set the record straight, there's no love lost between Gold and yours truly. The Westminster chimes play their tune halfway through. You were planning to drive us home, my grandmother points out, obviously annoyed, though whether by the interruption or the piecrust it's hard to say. The child should be in bed, she announces. Look at her eyes, like burnt holes in a blanket. But the inspector isn't really paying attention. Speaking of which? he asks politely, nodding toward the kitchen door, sniffing.

Though the farther you travel from it, the less difference it seems to make what's going on in there, the sauté pan upended on the floor, the glue fused to the stove lid, and Pook on the move, having successfully retrieved a duck. Without stopping to consider, Edwina takes off in pursuit, chasing him through the larder and into the hall, which she's surprised to find empty and dark. From the dining room comes the sound of laughter, a chiming of knives and forks and crystal, chair legs scraping against floorboards, chamber instruments tuning up. Gentlemen, a toast! To our fair hostess, and her most recent endeavor. Everything seems so far away, reduced in size, remote: the tiny fanlight, far off at the end of the hall, pitch-black and streaked with minuscule raindrops, each one blackly coruscating. It will take hours to get to the vestibule at this rate, and in any case Henny would appear to have beaten Edwina to the punch, if that's indeed who she sees inching along up ahead, a barely animate bundle of rags, redolent of sweat and burned glue.

As Edwina watches, the bundle pauses, looks back furtively over its humped shoulder, then disappears through a door Edwina's never noticed before, so perfectly do its edges blend into the surrounding paneling. She can hear faint barking, the sound of wind in the pines, clamoring voices, spoons beating little tin cups. On the hook to her right, her long-lost wool cape and Henny's plaid shawl; on the hook to her left, her husband's greatcoat and, below it, his mud-caked boots, a sprung mousetrap. In this house at least the mice seem able to come and go as they please.

The floor initially feels smooth under her feet, then oddly uneven, moist; what seem to be blades of wet grass are sticking up between her toes. No light to speak of, though Edwina finds she can just make out a familiar big shape loping toward what appears to be a distant woods, far ahead, as well as smaller shapes, spreading among the trees like spilled ink. Come back! Pook, come back! she yells, surprised to find herself on a narrow trail thickly layered with spruce needles, rose-pale, studded with lichen-ringed stones, crisscrossed at intervals by segments of deadfall, tiny black bugs swarming out of their powdery hearts. Luckily the rain seems to have stopped, though she can still hear it dripping from the eaves. *Plink plink plink.* Or perhaps it's merely a case of rain not being able to penetrate into this part of the house. As for the mice, there's no sign of them anywhere, or of their disgusting hoards of beans and nuts, their mewling babies, their nests of hair and dust. Instead huge pillared rooms of spruce extend on either side of her, lit by pearl-gray moonlight, a gauzy filamental light that seems to have been strung from spruce limb to spruce limb, just as spiders have strung their tingling webs across the path. Touched, Edwina thinks; touched, but not felt. The woods don't feel you, and any sense you might have of being observed by them is nothing more than your own need to be admired.

Her pace slows; the trail darkens, rises steeply, its needles replaced by a jumble of stones, the bed of a dried-up stream where she's forced to pick her way. Black smooth stones. Edwina holds her breath, listening. That faint rushing sound, as if wind approaches to stir the crowns of the trees. Only it's not wind, but a waterfall. Louder, louder—the trail disappears under the pool at its base, breaks apart into wavering disks of moonlight, quartz-flecked pebbles, a silvery school of trout fry scooting this way and that, midges. Ice-cold. An exquisite pain radiating from your feet into your calves, like the nerves of a dying tooth. Edwina leans down, cups her hands, drinks; never has any liquid seemed so pure, so capable of slaking not only the great thirst with which she's been suddenly overtaken, but even the metaphysical thirst that drives the Spiritualists to keep up their endless rattling at God's door.

The hem of her shift is sopping when she emerges on the other side, leaving the prints of her bare feet in the mud among Pook's pawprints, pencil-thin shoots of equisetum, fist-sized droppings. Our entire planet's laced with such trails, made by animals and appropriated by humans, living creatures drawn in ever-deepening grooves across the world's surface, deposited first one place, now another. In the pool a little frilled shadow swims away fast. *I have been with you always,* it whispers.

Ding a ding dong; quarter of. Everyone is getting restive, yet with the exception of my father, no one has the initiative to make a move.

Don't get me wrong, Mink, he says, looking at the inspector over his shoulder as he leaves his chair to let out Noodle, who's been whimpering and scratching at the swinging kitchen door. Mink, right? Some of my best friends are Jews. How handsome my father looks, his white shirtsleeves rolled to just below the elbow and a cigarette dangling from his lips! It drives my mother crazy when he does this, but for the moment she doesn't notice, her head lolling on the bent stem of its neck. Gracefully my father swings open the kitchen door and out billows a huge cloud of smoke, certainly more than could have been generated by one little incense cigarette. Jesus Christ, Dorothy, my father says. You'll have to excuse me, he adds, and we can hear the sound of water running in the sink. I don't believe this, we hear him saying, and then a thumping sound followed by a scraping, a hissing, a string of obscenities. (Thumping the flames with an oven mitt, scraping the incinerated meat-cake off the electric burner where it's been put to cook without a pan, dumping the thing, hissing, into the sink ...)

You'll have to excuse him, my mother echoes, for amazingly we're all still seated at the table as if nothing unusual is happening, despite the fact that everyone's face is contorted with coughing. More pie? she asks.

But the inspector shakes his head, an almost sorrowful gesture, then reaches into yet another of his many pockets and extracts a white cotton undershirt and a pair of white cotton underpants. Do you recognize these? he asks me. I'm sorry, he says to my mother, as if she's raised an objection, though with the exception of my sister, whose eyes are about to jump out of her head, everyone at the table is staring at the centerpiece. *Mrrrt mrrrt mrrrt* and a loud clanking as the exhaust fan starts up, then the storm door squealing open, the strange expelled breath of the pneumatic doorstop, a cold gust of air. The phone ringing. Recognize? I repeat stupidly, and again the inspector shakes his head. Have you seen these before?

Well of course: there's not a single middle-class girl who doesn't wear identical undergarments, though as my grandmother points out I am the lucky owner of a matched set of im-

ported days-of-the-week sateen panties which she herself gave
me (Lundi, Mardi, Mercredi, thanks a bunch) last Christmas.

Nope, my father's saying, we're all fine over here, Terry.
Then, dropping his voice: I don't know where she . . .

Could they belong to Miss Harbison? the inspector asks,
and my mother (a Perry Mason fan) informs him that he's leading the witness.

Maybe, I say. We all have our name sewn into jackets, hats,
things that could get lost at school, but unless you went to
camp, which Joy never did, not in your underwear.

The inspector nods, folds the garments back up, and re-
turns them to his coat. It's not a trial, he tells my mother.
Though there may be an inquest. Whoever these were, he says,
patting the pocket, I don't think they belonged to Mr. Benjamin
Franklin Gold. So what were they doing in his possession, that's
what I'd like to know.

Such ordinary-looking garments, but all you had to do
was put them in the wrong place, i.e. a man's house, and suddenly they weren't ordinary anymore. Though who could say
whether the fact that someone had hidden them in the weird
honey-colored chest in Benny Gold's living room altered the
truth about Joy's death. At what point does an accident stop being an accident?

At least he wasn't mean to Joy, I say.

A muffled crepitation on the far side of the pool, beyond
the towering umbrellas of the water parsley. Pook, Edwina whispers, is that you? But the noise is so purposeful, so plodding . . .
Go back, Edwina tells herself, now, before it's too late. The noise
gets louder, resolving itself into distinct sounds, footsteps, labored breathing; there's a rumbling fall of stones and then all at

once Edwina can see Henny, her small beak of a nose the only clear feature in an otherwise black and porridgey face.

Miz Moss, says Henny, the words indistinct and running together like overripe cheese. What you doing here? She seems unable to remove her eyes from Edwina, but a new dullness informs her stare, the way she holds her mouth slightly open, as if to suggest that she can find nothing to say to so negligible and loathsome a life-form. The woman's dangerous, Edwina concludes. She doesn't have my best interests at heart.

There's a sudden rustling in the water parsley, a moist sniveling. Lord have mercy! says Henny, whereupon Edwina, catching a glimpse of the familiar broad skull, the sweetly pricked ears, smiles, reassured. It's only Pook, she says. My darling! Though when she looks more closely what she sees approaching stiff-legged isn't really her dog but a horrible replica, the fur no longer lustrous, the entire bony armature vibrating, the rib cage squeezing from the bagpipe of the body a low humming growl.

Henny yanks hard on Edwina's arm, the blackened crust of her skin cracking as if she's been too long in the oven. Keep moving, she orders. Keemmmving: juices running from the pricked crust of her mouth. Don't slow down. She selects a stone, but Pook continues his advance, relentless, stiff-legged, eyes watery, muzzle matted and gluey with spit. It's only Pook, Edwina repeats. Pook would never harm a fly. Don't be a fool, says Henny. Whatever he was, he ain't now. Life won't stay put, and you can't stop it.

A little moonlight drains through the hemlocks, sowing the pool with diamonds. Suddenly the waterfall, which like any persistent background noise has been oddly inaudible, begins to roar. No time like the present, says Henny, casting about and selecting a fallen branch. She wades into the middle of the pool, her soiled garment hiked above her knees, the branch raised and ready. Long as we stay in the water, she says, gesturing, he can't hurt us. On account of hydrophobia, you mean? Edwina asks, but Henny only laughs. They all afraid of water, she says. The ones you summon with fire. She puts her arm around Edwina's shoulders to draw her closer, and when Edwina shudders, Henny pinches her once, hard. This ain't no time for airs, she points out. You with me, sister?

And she's right, for there's Pook again, if you could confuse that thing standing in the shadows on the other side of the pool, head lowered, lip curled, rib cage heaving, with sweet Pook. Eyes red like coals, the ears likewise, having become so thin, so transparent, the veins show through. Get onto your knees, says a man's voice. Quickly. And all at once he comes striding rapidly toward the pool from the dense woods to the north, twigs cracking under his boots—Simon Wingfield. His face, when he finally emerges into the dim light of the falls, is bright and appalled, the way a face looks when it hasn't had a chance to adjust to a situation but has come upon it cold, unable to believe that anyone confronted by a mad dog could stand there so calmly, knee-deep in a forest pool. Quickly, he repeats, lifting a rifle to his shoulder. Simon Wingfield, Edwina thinks. What is he doing here? You mustn't stand in the line of fire, he says, but Henny puts up both hands, admonitory.

No, she says, don't shoot. It would be a terrible terrible mistake. Can't you recognize her? Who? says Edwina, suddenly apprehensive. And then the doctor shoulders her out of the way, disgusted. Angrily he raises his rifle, takes aim ...

But what kind of world is this, Edwina thinks, where even the animals can be infected with something that turns their sweetness to malice? Where the soft muzzle that reposed on your lap can suddenly swing open revealing mucid fangs, foaming saliva, the wish to tear off your arm? Your own pet, your own daughter, as if a part of yourself might actually turn against you. Yet where did the idea of an infinitely divisible whole come from in the first place if not from the human brain, its infinite folds, infinite pathways, tracks and trails, surging rivers, tree-crowned hills and dark-green valleys, its grazing cows, rabid dogs, hay bales, iridescent fish leaping on sun-pricked hooks, rotting skin, quick sparks, waterfalls, all its glittering synaptic leaps . . .

In THE NIGHT NURSERY BOLTS OF MOON-light unroll through the windows and a large shadow, big and blockish, confronts the mother like her enemy. Or is it the Flemish doll's shadow climbing the faded rosebuds of my wall-paper? Not the mother's shadow, in any event. Of that much she can be certain.

Murder.

She whirls around. The voice is similar to the father's but infinitely tiny, the tiniest pinprick of sound, as if it comes from far far away. Beyond the window the world, held in place by a firm hand of sky.

Edwin, is that you?

Except the voice isn't coming from outdoors. No, it's somewhere in the room, emerging clear as crystal from within the dust snarl, dangerously close to one of the mother's unravel-ing feet. A solitary mouse, frailer than frail, quivering like a leaf on a winter beech tree. Beech leaves, hanging on long after all the other leaves have given up—the mother has always won-dered why they bothered. It isn't as if the sight of them com-pensates for the greater loss of a world cased in ice; indeed the presence of the beech leaves makes a mockery of persistence.

Mrrrt mrrrt mrrrt. Murderer, we salute thee, says the mouse, dipping the sleek wedge of its head in a slight ironic bow.

I'm sorry, the mother replies. How many times do I have to apologize ... Wait! Where do you think you're going? For all at once the mouse is skittering, a beech leaf in a breeze, across the floor.

How many times? That's easy. The number of mother-hood, reckoned from the heart's first quickening to its last quick release, says the mouse. Just so many times, no more, no less, lest thy children perish, murderer.

The mother makes a sudden lunge forward, but when she grabs the mouse's tail between her thumb and forefinger it snaps off at the base like a glass needle. When I put out cheese for you, she says, you were the one who wouldn't eat it. Some-thing like a tear runs down her cheek, a gummy secretion, the weeping of a meringue.

Death was never our wish, never, never! Never our wish for the mother's vigil to cease for a second. Flick of an eyelid, twinkling of an eye, and—poof!—a girlfriend gone. Each cas-tle in the air, its construction lavish, painstaking, and—poof! poof! poof! poof!—an entire family. The rules are the rules: decay is the wages of inattention. So shall my whole kind be de-stroyed, that a remnant of thee might be spared, little mother.

By now the mouse has made its way to the other side of the room, where it scrabbles for purchase on the hem of my yel-low quilt. What about me? I ask. You don't see any mother here, do you? My initial response, an indignant, almost angry sense of probity affronted, is fast eroding, changing into something less pure, as if the mouse itself, its frail ruined body, is scrab-bling for purchase on my heart.

Again I reach out, more delicately this time, and pry the mouse from the yellow fabric it clings to. Moonlight shines right through it, except in the shadowy places where the organs cluster.

The power of the motherless is almost absolute, it whispers. They are the lucky ones. The power of the motherless is the power of the unwatched; they are the ones for whom vigilance is irrelevant.

It weighs less than nothing, cupped there in my palm—just the faintest hint of pressure, the infinitesimal grip of its little claws. Holding on for dear life.

But I did have a mother once: she had brown eyes. Or maybe I'm remembering someone else's eyes. A stream (millrace?) that seemed wide as a river, and on the other side a tree, a yellow bird, the head of a doll. A man holding one hand, a woman the other. Pulling me up the bank. Maybe it's the doll's eyes I'm remembering. Except there they are again, big brown eyes, hovering above a juice glass with an orange rooster printed on it. After you faint you have to drink a little juice, honey. You need to restore your blood sugar. I was in a shop with high shelves and someone (Mr. Caruso?) was raising a special pole with grippers at the tip to pluck from the top shelf a box containing a jigsaw puzzle of an old mill. But the grippers didn't hold; down the box fell. It was dusty, the picture on the lid was faded, pieces of mill were raining across the floor, across the freezer filled with big mitten-shaped lumps of frost recognizable as last summer's Popsicles only from the inch or so of wood sticking out of them, half gallons of cheap ice cream, the kind with a picture of a colonial woman on the lid to make you think it's good when all you have to do is take one taste to know it's nothing more than puffed air, maybe a nut or a chip, something slimy, and then peas, green beans, potpies, peas, potato puffs, blueberries, peas, eggrolls, peas, french fries, peas, peas, peas!

Or maybe all I remember, really, is first happiness, then a rain of colors; first brown, then misery.

Dancing fire, dancing, dancing! Yes! the mouse says. The mother was a drinker, the father was a gust of wind. Fan the fire or blow it out. May thy limbs blacken and crumble to ash, O drinking mother! May the wind carry off thy sparks! Whatsoever the mother does not spit out, she consumes. Whatsoever the mother does not consume, she spits out. A rice seedling attacked by the fungus *Gibberella fujikuroi* will grow to several times its normal height and then die of Foolish Seedling Disease. Yet the plant isn't foolish, merely obedient, just as we are obedient to mouthrot, edema, viral papilloma. A black honeybee, a dropped comb, a hollow potato, a rattling window—why should they be omens of death? Why not find an omen of death in everything? Everything is as it's always been, little mother, which is to say, terrible.

The mouse is almost invisible now: when I try stroking the length of its body with my fingertip, it seems like what I'm stroking is my own palm. Please don't, I say. Please don't die.

But it's no use. Following a brief moment of complete weightlessness, so complete as to suggest weight's opposite, an eerie sense of my hand being swept quickly upward during that moment when more-than-nothing arises out of nothing, there comes the residual heaviness of less-than-nothing, the dead weight of flesh. The mouse reposes in my palm, its eyes opaque and bulging like twin specks of flyblow.

Down the hall in their mahogany four-poster sleep my parents, gently snoring, side by side. No foul rags stuffed in the hamper, no empty bottles hidden in the clock. Why that sense of time-out-of-joint, then, as when a vertebra swims to the left or right of the spine, taking with it the ribs, the lungs, the whole haunted body? T-4, fourth thoracic vertebra, the knowledge that anything you see in your mind will come to pass. Though of course you can never see the future, only look at the present and recognize it for what it is. Your sister's about to have a nosebleed; Noodle is about to drink some water. A length of moonlight laps over your parents' bodies; if you wrap your dead, you can trick yourself into thinking they're actually headed somewhere like packages.

... THOUGH I AM SORRY TO HAVE TO TELL YOU that this time there will be no YOU, this time I have no choice but to wash my hands of you, to deny you once, twice, three times, to turn a deaf ear to your disgruntled chorus of voices, to your furious refusal to understand how Edwina Moss, on whom you have come to rely for lavish and professional advice about matters pertaining to household management and cookery, could leave you so thoroughly in the lurch, now when you need me the most, when there is a duck waiting to be singed, a hungry husband rattling his newspaper in the parlor, a sullen toddler, a fractious scullery maid, a mysterious mold creeping across the bruised skins of the apples in the root cellar, an unsavory smell arising from the drain in the summer kitchen, oh how could Edwina Moss natter on and on about a fictitious family, as if their affairs might possibly have any bearing on your own industrious lives, as if she cannot sympathize with your outrage, whereas I understand it better than you will ever know, it is only that I understand as well the danger of assuming that a properly thickened roux guarantees happiness, only that I cannot ignore the little girl tossing and turning in the night nursery, moaning softly, not loud enough to awaken anyone but loud enough to startle the horses, to make them rear up on their hind legs, their mouths opening to expose ragged yel-

lowing teeth, pointed gray-pink tongues, loud enough to catch
the gypsy coachman's attention, to make him hurl his knife in a
swift silver arc across the room, to aim it for her heart, to wink,
to whisper, "Gertie Moss, Gertie Moss, I will play a song for
you and you alone on my xylo-bones, on my pee-flute, on my
wee valen-drum," and then to bend his head almost shyly and
begin unbuttoning his shirt, absurdly long with an endless row
of minuscule heart-shaped pearl buttons, while the girl touches
her own heart, and it is beating so fast she is ashamed,
ashamed—but where in God's name is the mother, for mightn't
we expect that her love for her child would alert her to the
lightest, most subtle withal nerve-chilling tug on that delicate
thread, on that ghostly relic of the original cord binding two
distinct souls, at the least sign of a beloved child's distress, and
while one might suspect that she has forgotten the words of Le
Ménagier de Paris ("well to keep the five bodily senses: the eyes
from foolishly looking, the ears from foolishly hearing, the
nostrils from too much smelling and delighting in sweet
odours, the hands from foolishly touching, the feet from going
into evil places"), it seems more likely that she is not so much
foolish as cursed with a darkly melancholic nature, such as is
frequently accompanied by a heightened imagination, a tendency to dwell in the realm of imagined pleasures or disasters
and thus to exclude all sensory proddings and pokings, the
moon lighting the rim of the copper mixing bowl, the chinging
of the wire whisk against its sides, the faintly metallic smell of
egg whites, the odd difference between the copper bowl's
smooth, placid coolness and the coiled, expectant coolness of
the whisk ... really! before we level judgment perhaps we
should recall that the fruit never falls far from the tree, that the
look of horror on the mother's face as she pours the corrupted

egg whites into the sink is identical to the expression on her daughter's face as she watches the gypsy peel back the two halves of his long white shirt, grab his nipples like knobs, pry open the twin casements of his wide brown chest, and play *ting ting ting!* on the sparkling ivory bars of his rib cage, *patapatapata-pan!* on the taut valentine-shaped head of his heart, while the cart and horses flatten into shimmering panels of silk, flutter and drift, flutter and drift, brushing against the girl's hot limbs, snagging ever so delicately on the fine hairs of her forearms, causing her to shiver, to tremble, her agony high-pitched and exquisite, her eyes opening wider and wider as the man's thing begins to rise from its hiding place between his legs, higher and higher, until it reaches his lips, at which point he yanks it loose at the root and lifts it, grayish pink and laced with veins and stiff as a poker, and plays it like a flute, and meanwhile there is the mother leafing nervously, anxiously, her fingers trembling with nameless dread, through cookbook after cookbook, hearing what she thinks is the squealing of wind caught in a window casing, and there is Gertie, sweat-drenched Gertie, MY Gertie, with her red crown of hair, her constellation of freckles across the bridge of her nose, her ... NO, it is too pathetic, too presumptuous, and why not admit at last to the ugly truth, that the authors of such books as this, having tended from the beginning to confound food and physic, cook and doctor, butcher and God, always end by advocating the superior claim of one life over another, whether to tempt the palate ("take your Pigg and hold the head down a payle of cold Watter untill strangeled") or to cure the plague ("take a Cock Pullet and pluck of the fethers of the taile or hinderpart till the rump be bare, then hold the bare of the said Pullet to the sore and the Pullet will gape and labour for life and in the end he will dye

..."), as if all I need do is profess mastery of my subject, give a name to the child's disease or the forest through which the army marches (anthrax, consumption, the Bloody Angle, Wilderness Tavern), and death itself will assume recognizable form, will no longer be everywhere present but contained instead in a symptom, an event, a tremulous tongue, a regiment burned alive, blood from the nose, corpses piled on corpses, will promote just such false hope, in short, as does each futile search through the books for that food either savory or sweet, cold or hot, a pleasure to the tongue or a challenge to the teeth, highly spiced or subtly flavored, which approaches the heart's desire, for that dish which when perfectly prepared (since your attempt at Oeufs à la neige ended in failure, and was in any event WRONG, too hodgepodge, too lacking in focus) will spring the trap of your apprehension, and are you guided by an unconscious understanding of that upon which the body's good health relies, the sailor's wild hunger for an orange? the anemic's thirst for red blood? or driven instead, as some experts would have it, by a perverse yearning for the object of your destruction, and WHY OH WHY can we not abandon the search altogether and deny the body's tyranny, cease to endlessly embellish on the garment, as if for our spirits to go unclothed would be to invite calamity, a vast whiteness through which nothing individuated shuttles, the snow outside my kitchen window but with no eye to see it nor ear to hear its almost soundless fall nor tongue to catch and taste it, only a pervasive white world in which nothing gets lost, nothing dies, a world, in fine, such as that which the anonymous author of *A Learned Dissertation on Dumpling; its Dignity, Antiquity, and Excellence, with a Word upon Pudding,* having first traced its origins (... "ſome added Marrow, others Plumbs"), has characterized as hopelessly corrupt, but which I've come to recognize, paging through book after book, as the only possible response to my terror: PUDDING WORLD, WHITE WORLD: the world I must make and enter, the world which sues to rob us of our garments, its name legion, WHITE-EAT, BLANC-MANGE, that staple of Victorian cuisine prodded by a finger of sunlight to tremble on the sideboard, but also staple of the sickroom, the nursery, bland and consolatory, designed to tempt the faltering palate, my own husband's choice whenever he would most painfully suffer the slings and arrows of our barbed union ("A Shape, Eddy dearest, if it's not too much trouble," standing there balefully, dolefully, not looking me in the eye in order to drive home his point, that no amount of ex-ertion on my part could begin to atone for the wrongs he has endured at my hands, as all the while Henny, she who I feel cer-tain despite the crystal clarity of my instructions is now glee-fully reading this document, would press upon him inedible sweets—they were, you know!—of her own devising) though my Gertie has always despised blancmange ... a bastard con-coction to begin with or at least as it appears in Le Ménagier ("... then bray great plenty of almonds and capons' guts"), a concoction neither meat nor sweet, just as Chaucer's mention of it in the Prologue seems promoted by his preceding descrip-tion of the Cook's ulcerous shin, and even as it approaches the form we know today it retains vestiges of its odd beginnings ("To make blomonge take one Pint of Milk and half a Hand-ful of picked Isinglass ...") which happens to be, I need not re-mind you, a gelatine prepared from the internal membranes of fish bladders, the very substance I've removed from my larder and am now preparing to test its "bloom," dropping threads of it first into boiling water, where it dissolves completely, then

into cold water, where it turns cloudy, then into vinegar, where
it swells and thickens into jelly, as if to mimic the actions of the
poor young woman in the fairy tale who coaxes forth from
nothingness the ardent body of her husband by fixing three
baths for him, one of water and milk, one of milk, and one of
rosewater, thereby bearing out history's darkest assumptions
about what goes on in a kitchen, "for whoever giveth all its
pleasure to a bear, a wolf, or a lion, that same bear, wolf, or lion
will follow after him, and so the other beasts might say, could
they but speak, that those thus tamed must be bewitched" . . .
and so the other inhabitants of the village might say, could they
but see me at work, could they but see the fiercety of my gaze,
the way in which the thick coils of my hair, having come un-
pinned, have been shoved back in great loops and swags like a
recently disturbed nest of copperheads, could they but see the
way in which I've shoved the sleeves of my white blouse high
above the elbows to wipe my brow with the flat of my forearm
like a field hand, my mouth set in a frown, could they but wander into that kitchen, lit only by the silver light of the moon,
ah! I have no doubt that could they but speak, had they not
themselves felt their blood first pouring, dissolute, through
their veins, then clouding up, then jelling, their limbs jelling
into place, mouths jelled open to reveal the quivering aspic of
their tongues, then they would damn me for a witch and thrust
me head first into my own white-hot oven, but not before
they'd snuck a little taste of sugar from the bowl, popped an almond or two between their moist lips, maybe even made the
mistake of wresting from the wreckage of the bedclothes Gertie's feverish body and carrying her off to a bona fide doctor in
whose care she would surely die, while her only hope, as YOU
at least know—YOU who must also know how sharper than a

serpent's tooth is your flagrant disregard of a dying mistress's wishes—lies in the hands of that woman who is now bringing a pot of water to boil and throwing into it, as Carême instructs, a pound of sweet almonds (imported from Spain) and approximately twenty bitter almonds (so-called due to the presence in their chemical composition of prussic acid), thus blanching them prior to setting them in a bowl of cold water "which renders them singularly white," WHITENESS being one of the two chief objectives, the other SMOOTHNESS, for as Carême exhorts the cook, "these delicious sweets, to be enjoyed, must be extremely smooth and very white, two qualities rarely found together," an observation I am bound to confess has always given me cause to wonder, for what of a woman's skin? . . . and while it would appear that Carême never married, there can be no doubt that his position as chief cook for the Czar Alexander, the Baron de Rothschild, Prince Talleyrand, von Metternich, would have brought him into contact with some of the most beautiful women of his day, would have provided him more than a glimpse of their smooth white shoulders, their smooth white arms, their smooth white foreheads, all bathed in the warm glow of candlelight, as meanwhile the gentlemen unfurled around them the smooth white yardage of diplomacy, their fingers lifting to their lips silver spoons in which reposed such smooth white issue of Carême's inspired creation as prompted one observer to suggest that the meekness of the Russian autocrat during the Conventions of 1814 might perhaps be explained by the excellence of the blanc-mange, nor on reflection does it seem unlikely that Carême would have found this very confluence of effects—skin and intrigue and sweetmeat—an affront, as if to dare suggest that anything in nature, even the Czarina's white arms, Metternich's

smooth tongue, could approach his genius, could justify the
metamorphosis into chyme of that dessert whose sublimely
conceived architecture had cost him many a sleepless night,
could justify the transformation of blancmange into a churning
pottage of gastric juices and clotted milk and fatty acids, nor
would there be any solace in the knowledge that at some future
time the tiniest speck of that original pudding, after having
been plucked up by the villi and propelled into the bloodstream, might finally emerge as an infinitesimal speck of
smooth white skin, for could it not as easily combine with ill-
favored elements to form a malignancy, a beauty mark gone
bad, the deadly melanoma whose taproot drives forth the soul,
and isn't this after all the cook's ultimate privilege, to dream the
food but not to have to eat it, never to witness the dream's subtle shift into nightmare, nor do I intend to devour the pudding
I am even now—as the clock strikes one and I once again mistake the demonic music coming from the night nursery for the
clock's creaking weights and pulleys, for the resonant humming
echo of its chime—demoniacally engaged in composing, my
hands tremulous as they rub the sieved almonds in a napkin,
and OH! those almonds are very white indeed, white as the
snow on the hillsides, white as the moon, white as pearls, as
bones, as the marble mortar in which I tremulously place them
and then, adding water a little at a time, pound them to a paste,
slowly, slowly, for this is a procedure requiring patience if the
paste is not to release its poisonous oils, a delicate procedure
requiring in equal quantities that great patience and its attendant capacity for lightning-quick action which is the hallmark
of all true cooks, to wait for the moment and when the moment has come to act, to know precisely when to lay a clean
napkin over a dish and pour the mixture through it, then to art-

fully wring the napkin so as to press through its weave every
last drop of the almond-flavored liquid, to make certain in
short that when at last the "milk," as Carême designates it, has
been combined with twelve ounces of sifted sugar, and when
this sweetened milk has been strained yet again through a clean
napkin, and when at last has been blended into it exactly one
ounce four grains of clarified isinglass, the resultant mixture
will be perfectly smooth and white, devoid of even the most
microscopic speck of blanched nut, the most apparently incon-
sequential grain of sugar, the most minuscule gelatinous lump,
will be in fact utterly without texture, without substance, almost, you might say, without material existence, so that you
might be tempted into thinking that to swallow it would be to
swallow nothing, to attempt communion not with the body
and blood of God's son but with the Holy Ghost itself, though
of course were you to choose instead to continue following
Carême's instructions, pouring the mixture into a mold bedded
in a tub containing fifteen pounds of cracked ice, you would
soon enough (in three hours, to be exact) find yourself confronted with a decidedly substantial object, the blancmange un-
molded in all its luminous glory on a serving plate, nor would
you have any difficulty understanding why Mrs. Beeton persists
in referring to such puddings sweepingly as "shapes," for while
it is true that jellymolds tend toward three basic types (the cas-
tle, the hat, the gemstone), and while these tend in their symmetry to assert the thin line between artificial and natural
effect, between the frieze's studied repetition of eggs and darts
and the crystal's mindless replication of shining facets, there
can be no doubt that these shapes defy description, nor that the
impression they convey is deeply unnerving, the mysterious
form assumed by that which ought to have remained formless

... so that the cook—after at last choosing from among her impressive collection the one mold that best applies to the architect's implied grandiosity of scale (a ribbed central dome surrounded by helmed towers and crenellated ramparts), the milliner's more humble touches (braided galloons, flower garlands, tasseled aiguilettes), while still radiating that hint of a mineral soul the sheer redundancy of which has served to act on her like the mesmerist's swinging watch on his hapless subject, or like the large snowflakes now tumbling past the kitchen window—the lonely, sorrow-worn cook suddenly finds her original zeal for the project so thoroughly replaced by a ponderous fatigue, by such an overwhelming inability to keep her eyes open one second longer, that, the mold finally consigned to the ice, she sinks into an uneasy slumber, her head resting heavily in the nest of her arms, her arms on the tabletop, and meanwhile the vast clockworks of the universe continues its ceaseless movement, crystal linking with crystal, atom with atom, the blancmange beginning to set, the snowflakes to tumble faster, the very air around her to thicken, to grow cold, chilling her to the marrow, so that when, at last—at LONG LONG last—she hears that familiar voice, when at long last she hears the voice of her daughter crying out to her, she finds it impossible to move, to lift so much as a single finger (though perhaps the paralysis is merely an illusion, for surely the ability to discern motion rests in the body's sense of itself as discrete from its surroundings, and she's by now lost all such powers of discernment, her struggle to respond being the spirit's struggle to distinguish itself from ether, to pull itself like a conjuror's bouquet of flowers out of thin air ...), oh! her efforts are so pathetic and yet, finally, so dauntless, so utterly informed by her boundless love for Gertie, that what she somehow manages to

summon into action is not her own living body but the watery
contours of a ghost, alerted perhaps by the very fact of her
body's life, the ghost of the illustrious Antonin Carême in fact,
condemned to witness the wages of his culinary arrogance
played out again and again at the hands of rank amateurs, to
guide like Dante's Vergil the mournful damned through the
landscapes of their own infernal creation, a slender and lissome
ghost with a high smooth brow and dark curling hair, sharp
black eyes and a sensual mouth, a handsome ghost even, whose
fate was sealed when he was no older than Gertie and his poor
father left him at the Paris city gate ... yes, it is Antonin
Carême, elegant and vaguely reluctant, who appears as if out of
nowhere to whisper into her ear, *suis-moi, vite! vite!* and it is Antonin Carême who places his ghostly hand on her shoulder, an
almost imperceptible pressure, like the remembered touch of
her husband, and then the heat of his breath on her neck, his
fingers slipping down to caress her breast, but when she twists
to see his face she discovers that the air has filled with white
spinning flakes—*vite! vite! vite!*—and that where once were walls
and stove and table there is only whiteness, spinning and
swirling whiteness, a raging blizzard, and she is unaccountably
on her feet, her feet in heavy boots trudging through drifts of
snow, and she is unaccountably wearing a heavy black cloak,
and at her side there is a man she has never seen before who is
urging her to hurry, telling her there is no time to lose, that her
daughter's life hangs in the balance, that her husband is dying,
and when she tries to turn back (because of course the house
must be somewhere behind them, because she cannot for the
life of her imagine what force might have prompted her to leave
her daughter alone in an empty house, to leave the house when
at any minute might arrive the long-awaited letter from her

husband), the man grabs her hand and draws her forward, *en avant! dépêche-toi, ma chèrie!*, draws her deeper and deeper into the drama of the storm, as if to insist that the sole drama worth attending to is OUT THERE, not in the house, not ... HERE, OH NO, NEVER HERE, NEVER IN THIS WRETCHED NURSERY where the Flemish doll sits forever propped in her little wooden chair, the expression on her porcelain face so maddeningly obtuse that with each renewed glance at it all hope of rescue evaporates, and how profound your hatred of that obtuse face, of that matted wig, which despite what Papa said in no way resembled my own beautiful hair, my hair the precise color of both the butterfly weed waving in the summer fields and of the monarchs hovering above it, my red hair I brushed one hundred strokes every morning and every evening until that ill-starred night when the fever loosened it at the roots and it fell out, every last strand of it, only to grow back coarse and black, nor could any amount of brushing coax from it the luster of the vanished locks, nor could the small green hatbox Papa brought back from a business trip to London (with a perfect replica inside of my dead Mama's bonnet, complete with midnight-blue, star-embroidered veil and an actual sky-blue linnet roosting on its rim) compensate, nor did I ever recover from my sense of outrage that he'd thought it possible I would want to wear a bird with glass eyes on my head, as if I could ever forget, or uncover, in the long weeks of my convalescence, anything other than an endless parade of napkin-draped delicacies on my bedtray ... SHAME ON YOU! oh, unspeakable shame, to let yourself touch or be touched by anything, anyone, when you understood the consequences, to have imagined even for one second that it was love which brought a creature like Gertie into the world when it was nothing more than an accident, the momentary collision of two bodies, any hint of real tenderness merely that of inflamed, tender skin, nor should you allow yourself to be misled by the husband's urgent grip on his wife's shoulders, by the urgent pull of her most deeply hidden muscles, for only afterward comes the dark recognition which is named love, which dares admit how dreadful is the quickening of a new spirit, how base the agent of its conception, doomed to cherish that which has already been, by such agency, betrayed ... POOR POOR THING! and yet who is to say whether I am moving away from Gertie or toward her, for even though the storm is abating, even though the sky (the ceiling?) is growing lighter, more translucent, and even though I can begin to see tall vague shapes (trees? pillars? their placement and their width regular enough to suggest the latter) I have no sense of where I am, only that terrible sense of either impending or unrealized loss which kept me awake in the first place, only the spectral presence at my side of Antonin Carême, whose terror now seems to overmatch my own, whose hand suddenly extends to shield my gaze from—what? a shadowy movement up ahead, something flapping or beating like a wing? a flap of cloth attached to a tree? but he hurries me past it, whatever it is, faintly iridescent like the wing of a crow, so that all I'm left with is the briefest tug of recollection, the sun shining on brass instruments, a dog yapping, and surely there can be no reason to weep so why then am I weeping, tears running down my cheeks, and what is it that has left a blotched and intermittent trail there in the snow at my feet, and how is it possible to hear anything over the howling of the wind, and what is that smell, and WHAT IS THAT SMELL? for it is like nothing I've ever smelled before, though there are hints in it of the bedroom, of the kitchen, a sensory conflation less explicable than that of whiteness and smoothness, of the drifting snow through which I'm trying to make my way, for example, though I'm no longer certain that what I've been walking through, what's been flying toward me, is in fact snow, but something more like dust, like ash, clouds of dust stirred by my boots, large lacy fragments of ash drifting past my face, and *yes*, of course, how could I be so stupid, for obviously we're walking along a slightly winding road, its surface thick with dust and ash, a narrow road through a mean and gloomy woodland, through the kind of stunted forest which springs up after the virgin timber has been removed, vine-strangled alder saplings and dwarf firs twisting from its floor, a network of rank black streams, of blighted watercourses turning on themselves to produce sodden, bush-studded swamps, a seemingly endless road through a seemingly endless waste, rendering futile any concern for chronology, rendering futile any speculation as to when snow became ash, when moon became sun, an infernal turnpike which, the moment we've abandoned every hope of destination, all at once deposits us at a crossroads, and there on the left, partly hidden by the sickly vegetation, a ruined building, its damp-swollen sills choked with weeds, its windowpanes wide-open mouths with jagged shining teeth, the yard around it charred black at intervals and at intervals marked with gleaming white knobs and rods and tusks, flies buzzing around piled horse droppings, a few flowers, yellow ones mainly, blighted and drear, and everywhere an unearthly silence, a silence the intensity of which suggests a hovering watchful presence, almost as if I've risen up out of myself to assume the role of menacing observer, almost as if I'm still in my kitchen, and before my very eyes the smooth white shape from which I've gone to such pains to remove all impurities has proved ultimately contaminated, almost as if it is the shadow of my own enormous hand that slowly descends, slowly, slowly, and ...*attend!* Carême whispers, finally releasing his grip on my wrist to climb stealthily onto the rotten porch, and *qui vive?* he whispers, reaching for the door when suddenly it swings open as if by its own volition and out pops a soldier boy like a bird from a clock, his skinny arm holding aloft a white scrap of cloth and his skinny white face contorted, sobbing, his rosebud mouth working like the vent of a hen to produce a scrambled egg of speech—"Don't mean no ain't no more threat than only please God don't let on the Old Man whittles deserters' spines to toothpicks and can't the lady see I'm too young to die not there leastways"—pointing to the right, to where the road once again disappears into the surrounding woods, to the very source of the dull rumbling we've been hearing for some time now, a rumbling intermittently punctuated with loud bursts of noise and "them woods is crawling with Johnnies" the boy sobs, by which I understand him to mean Lee's army, but when I try to draw him out on the subject he merely collapses onto a cracker box, then hides his head in his hands, and when I try to comfort him as I might Gertie, stroking his lank white-blond hair back from his forehead, I see lice crawling along his scalp, or possibly something worse, larger, more like ants, a ceaseless scurrying, brush them away! quick! quick! yet with each stroke of my hand their frenzied activity increases, hundreds of dark bodies which seem to pour in and out of the follicles at the base of the hair shafts, the hair itself now coming loose in lank white clumps and the thin layer of skin across the scalp also loosening, slipping beneath my stroking fingers, so that when I pry the cupped palms from the face what I see instead of eyes and nose and mouth are four gaping holes, a black wind rushing foully out of them, and

WHAT HAVE I DONE? for all at once my own complicity is undeniable, nor is it possible any longer to feign innocence, to believe that to entertain a fear is to render it impotent,
that to imagine peril is to secure immunity, that to create a
world is to assume control over what will live and die in it, as if
I've only just now discovered that it is not such power of choice
which lies within my grasp, but the skeletal limbs of the gibber-
ing dead (your own skeleton rising to assail the surface of your
body, its noble contours every day more and more ascendant,
every day the flesh more thoroughly put to the rout), and OH
GERTIE! WHERE OH WHERE—but Carême won't
allow me to continue, I must suppress all further outpourings,
for save in those instances when the soul's eternal perdition is at
issue, as in his own case, the language of the dead can only be
comprehended by the dead, and any attempt at communication
on the part of the living, no matter how ardent the plea, how
clever the contrivance, will come to naught, will render incom-
prehensible whatever meager store of information the dead
might strive to impart, news of a passing caravan, for example,
from which so persistently issued the unmistakable sound of
physical distress that the dying soldier, overmastering his fear
of robbery at the hands of the stretcher bearers, tried to mount
onto it as it sped by, only to have the coachman hurl back at
him curses, and an object which he took for a rock, though no
rock was ever so artfully sculpted, hard as bone yet resembling
less a skull than a tender human countenance, an object even
you—YES YOU!—must surely recognize, you whose tire-
some, slavering presence is all that remains to mock me now
that I too am dead, cast into God-knows-what species of un-
ending torment, or merely extinguished all at once like a lamp,
having coveted it avidly enough, dressing and undressing it

while at the same time referring to me with smug condescension as its mama, as if by such means you might tempt me into an alliance, might convince me to follow your lead, taking up knitting needles and pastel yarns, as if I were not abundantly aware of the difference between the quick and its copy, between skin and china, as if (and why not assign you the role of confessor, for didn't you seek after it diligently enough while I was alive?) during the months of my childhood spent in blessed convalescence, when I removed the doll's wig to spit into the waiting cavity of its head fragments of partly chewed veal, or when I slit its kid belly open and scooped away the stuffing, leaving a hollow place in which to deposit wads of bread, nuts, and raisins, all material too explicit to consign as I could liquids to the chamber pot, I was not mimicking in that act the mama bird dropping worms down her nestlings' throats, the lioness regurgitating raw meat for her cubs, indeed I was not playacting at motherhood but rather grooming myself for sainthood, taking for my model none of the abstinent young ladies ("The Brooklyn Enigma," "The Derbyshire Damsel," "The Welsh Fasting Girl") so fervently admired by those Spiritualists with whom the woods around Moss Cottage are crawling, but St. Catherine of Siena herself, who was said to have eaten a mere handful of herbs each day, occasionally jamming a twig down her throat to bring up the residue, St. Catherine who did not so much deny appetite as transform it, exchanging hunger for food with hunger for God ... YET WHAT IS THE USE, why exchange one hunger for another when they are the same, the deadly forest deeper and deeper into which Carême now draws me, everything swathed in blinding white smoke, wisps and scarves of it escaping above the treetops, bullets hitting the dust-caked floor like the first drops of a heavy rain, but a rain that serves to ignite rather than to quench, thousands of bright sparks set loose with each burst of rifle fire, smoldering and then catching in the underbrush, your house is on fire, YOUR HOUSE IS ON FIRE!

Look for these other novels by Kathryn Davis

Versailles

"Splendid. . . . Marie Antoinette's very much alive here, and she's magnificent."

— Stacey D'Erasmo, *New York Times Book Review*

"Elegant. . . . A rich and strange meditation on the girl whose destiny was to be misunderstood by her people and by history."

— Katharine Weber, *Los Angeles Times Book Review*

The Girl Who Trod on a Loaf

"Magnificent, a bravura performance of grand imagination and fierce intelligence. . . . Kathryn Davis is a writer of original gifts and haunting power." — Ephraim Paul, *Philadelphia Inquirer*

"Brilliant. . . . *The Girl Who Trod on a Loaf* is heated, dramatic, grand in its ambition."

— Maggie Paley, *New York Times Book Review*

Back
Bay
Books

Available in paperback wherever books are sold